HAZEL
tree
farm

the
SECRET
tunnel

Alma Jordan lives on a farm in County Meath with her husband Mark and son Eamon. After a successful career in marketing and communications, she founded the award-winning social enterprise AgriKids in 2015 to spread the message of farm safety to children in a fun and engaging way.

Alma grew up on a farm in County Kildare, and the Hazel Tree Farm series features lots of real-life stories from her childhood, as well as moments shared by the children she meets through her work today. This is the second book in the series, after *Blue the Brave*.

ALMA JORDAN

ILLUSTRATED BY MARGARET ANNE SUGGS

THE O'BRIEN PRESS
DUBLIN

DEDICATION

To all the AgriKids I have met over the years. Your enthusiasm for farming and your stories from home have inspired and motivated me. This one's for you!

ACKNOWLEDGMENTS

To my family, Mark and Eamon (and of course our beloved pooch Benji) as well as my parents, Mags and Dave, sisters Emily and Louise, and brother Derek. I have kept you all with me as I wrote this story. You provided me with company and comfort, and this book would not be possible without you.

First published 2023 by
The O'Brien Press Ltd,
12 Terenure Road East, Rathgar, Dublin 6, D06 HD27, Ireland.
Tel: +353 1 4923333; Fax: +353 1 4922777
E-mail: books@obrien.ie; Website: obrien.ie
The O'Brien Press is a member of Publishing Ireland.

Published in:

DUBLIN
UNESCO
City of Literature

Growing up with
O'BRIEN
obrien.ie

ISBN: 978-1-78849-333-8

Printed in the UK by Clays Ltd, Elcograf S.p.A.

The Secret Tunnel receives financial
assistance from the Arts Council

CONTENTS

Chapter 1

Calamity Calves

'No, no, no!' wailed Peter, as a buckarooing calf suddenly made a sharp right turn away from the herd. 'You're going the wrong way!'

Peter extended his arms as far as they would go to guide the cheeky youngster back to the other calves, who by now were getting far too excitable for his liking.

As he lowered his arms once again, his long cattle stick dragged beside him in the mud. This wasn't how Saturday mornings were supposed to go. It was still the summer holidays, after all, and right now he should be curled up on the sofa with a massive bowl of Chocco Puffs watching his favourite TV programmes on the SoFun Network. Shows like *Billy & Frank: Crime-Busting Pups* or *The Mighty Kidz: Superheroes.*

Instead, he was out in the lashing rain trying to move a herd of young calves who, quite frankly, had zero sense of direction. Or, for that matter, zero sense of anything.

He had considered bringing Blue, his champion border collie. She was a top animal herder, but these calves were very young and only accustomed to people. Seeing a dog, even one as lovely as Blue, could cause panic and even more mayhem.

Blue and Peter were the local sheepdog trial champions, and they had represented Ballynoe at the county final. Even though they hadn't won, they were highly commended, and their success was the talk of the county for many weeks after.

Now it wasn't just Peter trying to guide the giddy calves to their new paddock – it was a family affair.

Peter's little sister, Kate, dressed in her bright-yellow rain-coat, stood sodden and miserable halfway down the lane. She leaned against the hedge, trying to get some shelter. Her job was to 'block the gap'; to stop any calves wiggling through the small opening in the hedge behind her. She had a cattle stick of her own, which she held limply by her side.

'How much longer?' she called out again. 'I am freeeeeez-ing!'

'Not much longer, Kate!' Mam called back, trying to keep the mood upbeat. 'You just stay where you are. You're doing a great job!'

Not believing a single word her mother said, Kate pouted and smacked the ground with her stick, splattering her wellies with mud as she did so.

'Why is my job the most boring of all?' she whined to no one in particular.

If she was a calf, she would have no interest in the field

behind her anyway. It was boggy and wet, full of reeds and mossy grass. Nothing like the beautiful, lush green pasture that awaited them at the end of the lane. Why couldn't they just hurry up and get to the good stuff?

Kate normally loved helping with the animals – she wanted to be a vet when she grew up, like Mam – but moving calves had to be the worst job on the farm. And if these animals (and people) didn't do what they were told, they would all be in trouble with Dad, whose normally jolly nature was nowhere to be seen on this miserable Saturday morning.

'Peter, you have to stay *RIGHT*!' Dad was pointing his finger frantically to the right just in case anyone was not sure what he meant by … '*RIIIIIGGGGHHHHTTTTT*!'

'I know!' Peter called back. 'I'm trying, Dad, but they keep moving the other way!'

Peter lifted his stick in one sudden motion to wave the calves on, but they could sense his cross mood and they didn't like it. Not one bit. Instead of moving on, all eleven of them panicked and took off in a gallop, veering sharply right into a tangle of briars and branches. Soon they were completely stuck, very upset, and mooing loudly for all to hear.

'Oh no …' Peter groaned.

'Oh no …' Mam whispered under her breath.

'Well, that's *thorn* it!' Kate called out, grinning at her own joke.

Dad was furious. 'Get them out of there, Peter!' he blasted from the top of the lane.

Mam didn't want her son getting tangled in briars with a bunch of young, skittish animals, so she ran to his side. 'You stay there, Peter. I'll go in. If I can get around them, I will push them back out to you. Remember, when they come out, send them *right*, towards Dad.'

Peter watched as poor Mam fought her way through, the brambles scratching and scraping her legs and arms.

This wasn't how Marian Farrelly planned to spend her Saturday either. As the local vet for Ballynoe, she had plenty of her own work to be doing. The Reillys' cat was about to have kittens. And she had to take care of a poorly hamster called Charlie who had escaped from his hutch and nibbled his way through a whole bag of hamster snacks.

'Go on, go on, you little monkeys.' Mam spoke gently to the calves as she tried to coax them out. But instead of turning the way she wanted, the silly sods moved further back until there was nowhere else to go. Now they were in an even bigger mess and an even bigger panic.

Mooooo Moooo Moooooooooo! they cried.

'Oh, for goodness sake,' Mam muttered.

Kate shook her head and rolled her eyes.

'What's the holdup?' Dad called from down the lane, his mood not getting any better. 'What is going on?'

Peter gave a thumbs-up. 'They're coming, Dad! Is the gate ready?'

He turned to his mother, knowing it was now his job to rally the troops as Mam was starting to look fed up. 'Come on, Mam. We've got this.'

Mam used her stick to smack and flatten the branches and overgrowth. Soon she had made a path wide enough for her to reach the panicked calves. By now they had stopped mooing and were watching this human with great curiosity. One, with the number '1360' on her yellow ear tag, licked her nostril as she stared.

All the calves had to do now was to turn back around and they would be facing the path to freedom.

'Come on, you lot,' grumbled Peter under his breath. 'It's not rocket science.'

Mam continued to move carefully towards them, gently rubbing her hand along their necks and heads.

'Come on,' she whispered as she looked into each set of big brown eyes. 'Let me help you out of this mess.'

Mam gently pushed '1360' away from her, prompting the calf to turn her head and then her whole body. She was now able to see the opening she had come through, and without any hesitation, she headed towards the laneway. The others dutifully followed.

'Finally!' Peter smiled and got ready to move the herd in

the right direction.

Mam pulled herself free from the briars, making sure she stayed close behind the calves. She dipped her head to avoid the low-hanging branches. But as the last calf emerged onto the laneway, it brushed past a thick briar, jutting out from the side. It dragged the branch forward as far as it could go, making it swing back at great force just as Mam was approaching.

SLLLLLLLAAAAAAAPPPPPPP!

'Ouch!' Mam cried out, as the branch slapped her hard in the leg.

Peter winced, but there was no time to check if his mother was ok. The calves were now back on the path, and Peter was in action mode. Raising his arms – slowly and calmly this time – he veered the animals right. Finally, things were going to plan.

Dad, happy to see the animals back on the path, looked over to see his wife standing by the bushes, patting her throbbing leg.

'Marian, you're too far behind!' he called out grumpily. 'Catch up! They'll scatter in all directions if you don't keep them tight.'

Feeling flustered, Mam took off in the direction of the calves. 'G'wan, g'wan, hoop hoop!' she shouted, waving her hands.

'Don't run!' Peter warned in a loud whisper. 'You'll scare them again.'

Mam slowed down, throwing him an exasperated look. 'I always hated moving cattle,' she said through gritted teeth. 'I remember doing it when I was your age, and your grandad would get so grumpy.' She brushed a wet lock of hair out of her face, her leg still stinging from being slapped by the branch.

'Me too,' said Peter softly, hoping he was making his mam feel better. 'But we're nearly there. Let's just get them safely to Dad.'

'That's it, Kate,' Dad was shouting, his attention now on his daughter. 'You stay right where you are.'

By this stage, Kate had been 'staying right where she was', guarding the same gap in the hedge, for nearly an hour. The rainwater was running down her face. Some drops had reached her neck and made their way inside the three layers of clothes she had on. Her teeth chattered with the cold.

'Kate, remember, you *have* to block that gap,' Dad shouted. 'If they go towards you, hold your stick up and that'll turn them towards me.'

'Finally something to do!' Kate called back.

She stood tall and braced herself for her big part. She lifted her stick as if it were a mighty sword, holding it out in front of her. 'You shall not pass!' she said in a commanding tone.

Peter rolled his eyes while Mam grinned.

'Stop being so dramatic,' Peter called out to his sister. But he knew now was not the time to take his eyes off the job.

Calf 1360, who was obviously the leader of this crazy crew, suddenly glimpsed the tiny opening in the hedge where Kate stood. She made a bolt for the gap in spite of the bright-yellow human guarding it. Thinking this was a great idea, two more bovine brainiacs followed, and soon all three were heading straight for Kate.

'Peter,' his father roared, 'keep them right! Right! Go *right*!'

'I'm *trying*!' Peter shouted back defensively.

All the sudden shouting spooked the other eight calves, who also took off in full flight in Kate's direction.

'Daaaaaaaad ...' pleaded Kate, 'they're coming! What do I do?' She tried to hide behind her stick.

'Wave your stick!' shouted Dad. 'WAVE YOUR STICK!'

Trying to look braver than she felt, Kate waved her stick in front of her. 'Shoo, shoo!' she shouted. 'Get away!'

Suddenly Mam ran wide to the left, her outstretched arms creating a shield between the calves and Kate. Peter followed her lead.

Seeing her mother and brother coming to her aid, Kate felt more confident and took a step forward, her stick in the air.

With their path blocked, the calves skidded to a stop. Their hooves sprayed fresh mud all over Kate, Peter and Mam.

'Arrrrrgh!' Kate shouted in disgust. 'Anyone got a tissue?'

But no one was listening to her. The calves were on the

move once again, with Peter and Mam trying to keep up. Luckily, the animals decided to pirouette back towards Dad, finally heading for the field gate.

Determined to get this job done, Kate took up her position alongside Peter and Mam. She walked to the right; Peter was staying left, leaving Mam happily in the middle. This was their walk to glory. All they had to do now was to keep this situation steady and under control.

Soon they reached the gate. In no time, the calves would be safe in their new home in the front paddock of Hazel Tree Farm.

'That's it,' said Dad, finally sounding calm. 'Keep them coming, we're nearly there.'

The calves were now trotting towards Dad, who was holding the opened gate with his left hand. His right arm was outstretched. He was gripping a stick, which gave him additional arm length, preventing any calves escaping to his right.

Peter copied his dad, extending his arms to create more length. He took a deep breath and focused on the calves in front of him. Just like herding sheep, he knew only too well they had to get the balance of speed versus timing. Moving too fast at the wrong time was disastrous, they had seen that. Just keep it slow and steady.

He was concentrating and staring so hard at the rumps of the eleven little calves that he didn't see the pothole that lay in his path.

SPPPLLLAAAAAATTTT!

Poor Peter was face down on the wet, mucky, stony lane.

'Owwwww!' he cried out. His hands and face were filthy, and his knees were badly scraped.

Mam pulled Peter up, while Kate kept the procession moving forward. They were a team now, and their prize was in sight.

'That's it … That's it …' Dad's words came slow and steady. The calves were just a few feet from him, with calf 1360 leading the way.

'That's it, girls,' whispered Peter as he limped along beside them. 'You're nearly there.'

'Not much longer,' breathed Mam.

'*Please* just go in the field,' begged Kate.

Spotting the luscious green grass that awaited her, calf 1360 took off in full flight through the open gate. The others followed, bucking, leaping and skipping as they did so.

With a big grin and a tremendous feeling of pride, Dad closed over the gate, sliding the latch into place. He paused to watch the eleven heifers playing happily. The rain had stopped, and the sun had finally come out. A perfect morning.

'Now, that wasn't so bad, was it?' Dad asked, turning towards the three sodden, muddy figures behind him. Peter's hands were bloodied from his fall, Mam's leg stung, and Kate's face and clothes were speckled with dried mud droplets.

'Oh no, are we too late?' The man's voice came from down the lane.

The Farrellys turned to see their neighbours Eamon and Maggie Cooper, who had come to help with the move. They wore sensible overalls and wellington boots and carried long cattle sticks.

'Oh, we've missed it.' Maggie sounded disappointed before spotting Peter's bloodied hands. She rushed over, taking a tissue from her pocket.

'We said we'd be over as soon as that rain had passed,' said Eamon.

'Daaaaad!' cried the children in unison.

'We could have used their help,' said Mam.

'I, em ... Well, emmm ...' Dad struggled to find the words. 'I thought it would be something nice we could do together, as a family.'

But the children weren't buying it.

'This has *not* been a good day,' remarked Kate to Eamon and Maggie.

'Not *one bit* good,' added Peter, trying to avoid Maggie's tissue.

'Ahh, it's always a good day when new animals arrive,' said Eamon, watching the calves over the paddock fence.

By now they had settled and were starting to graze. Some

were even lying down, which was a sign of contentment.

'Look at that!' said Eamon, putting his arm around the children. 'This is a big day. It's been over twenty years since cattle were at Hazel Tree.'

'I remember when I was a young woman, coming to Ireland and seeing all the wonderful cows, looking so healthy and happy,' said Maggie with a smile. 'Cattle have always thrived on this land, and so have those of us lucky enough to live here.'

Kate looked on, her irritations fading away as she watched the calves. She remembered how lucky she felt to live on a farm surrounded by animals.

'I'll be down in a couple of days with some medicine,' said Mam. 'With all this rain, nasty parasites can thrive in that grass, and I don't want them picking up something.'

'Some of them had ringworm when they arrived,' added Dad. 'We treated them with iodine.'

'What's ringworm?' asked Peter, looking a bit worried.

'It's a skin infection,' said Mam. 'Can be fairly common in cattle, but it's easily treated.'

'Can people catch it?' asked Kate.

'Yes, they can,' said Maggie, who was now trying to rub the mud from Kate's face with the same tissue she used on Peter. 'That's why we always wash our hands after touching these animals.'

'You should have hung up a holly branch in their shed,'

Eamon said with a chuckle. 'My mother used to say that it prevents ringworm.'

Kate wasn't sure which was more gross, a case of ringworm or whatever she was going to catch from Maggie's tissue.

'Right,' said Mam. 'Let's leave these ladies to settle in and get ourselves on the right side of a cup of tea.'

'Absolutely,' agreed Maggie. 'And I know of a certain tin box with the most delicious goodies.'

'Maggie's Treat Tin!' Peter and Kate shouted together, high-fiving each other.

'You got it,' laughed Maggie. 'Caramel squares, rocky road bites, and fresh scones hot out of the oven. I even have some homemade raspberry jam.'

'We'll be with you soon,' said Dad, as Maggie, Mam and the children walked away.

He and Eamon stayed for a final look at the new calves. Their little tails swished from side to side as they happily grazed on the fresh, green grass.

'Have I done the right thing, Eamon?' Dad asked, sounding unsure. 'Will this be enough to keep the farm going?'

Lately the value of sheep had gone down, and some farms were struggling to make ends meet. With animals to be fed and bills to be paid, things were tight at Hazel Tree. There seemed to be less money each year and no signs of things improving. Dad was worried that buying these new cattle was too much. What if their value also fell? It could make things so much worse.

'Hazel Tree always provides,' Eamon said kindly. He had worked with the Farrelly family for most of his life, as well as running his own chicken farm next door with Maggie. 'I remember your dad asking me the same thing. This land is special, and you are following a long line of great farmers whose instincts were always strong.'

As Dad and Eamon spoke and watched the cattle in the paddock, they hadn't noticed Peter listening close by. He had crouched down to fix the crumpled sock in his welly boot and overheard what they were saying.

What does that mean, 'keep the farm going'? he thought in alarm. *Is Hazel Tree in trouble?*

Not wanting to be seen, Peter crept away and caught up with the others.

'Come on, slowcoach!' Mam called to him as they headed up the road to Cooper's Cottage.

Peter was going as fast as he could, but his achy knees were slowing him down. And despite Maggie's best attempts with the tissue, he was still covered in mud.

The noise of a car coming from behind made him move to the side of the road. A huge Mercedes-Benz was travelling in his direction. As it got closer, it slowed down before coming to a complete stop. The window on the passenger side glided down.

A well-dressed lady with a silk scarf and bright-red lipstick smiled at him. An equally well-dressed man in a suit and tie was driving. In the back seat was a boy who looked about the same age as Peter. He was staring down at a mobile phone. As he momentarily took his gaze away from the screen, he looked Peter up and down, and a slow smirk spread across his face.

'Excuse me,' the lady asked, 'can you help us with directions, please?'

'Really, Mummy,' came the voice from the back, 'it looks like he can't even wash himself, let alone tell us where to go.'

'Stop it, Simon,' the man said, glaring back over his shoulder. Then he turned back around to speak to Peter. 'Sorry about that. We were all up very early this morning.'

'Simon' in the back seat made a loud *humphhhhh* noise and went back to his mobile phone.

Peter was amazed. None of the other kids in his class had their own phone.

The lady continued, slightly embarrassed. 'We're looking for Greenway Manor. It seems that our phones have no signal here.'

'That's 'cause *nothing* works here,' the voice from behind grumbled. 'Only this rubbish game on my rubbish phone.'

There was something about this Simon that was making Peter nervous.

'Emmm, yes, you are on the right road ...' Peter stuttered.

'Is everything ok?' Thankfully Dad and Eamon arrived.

'Oh, great, there's more of them,' Simon hissed.

'Hello! I'm Diane Sinclair,' the lady said, ignoring the grumblings from behind. 'This is my husband, Derek. We're moving into the area and seem to have gotten ourselves a little bit lost.'

'You are very welcome to Ballynoe,' said Eamon, tipping his cap. 'I'm Eamon Cooper, and this is David Farrelly and his son, Peter.'

'Where exactly are you looking for?' asked Dad.

'Greenway Manor,' continued Diane. 'Our movers are already there waiting for us. We made a wrong turn, and now our sat nav can't find its way back. It's really quite a predicament.'

'Welcome to the countryside,' laughed Eamon, 'where unfortunately technology has not quite fully arrived.'

Eamon's warmth made everyone relax, and the Sinclairs smiled warmly, except for Simon, whose dour expression hadn't lifted at all.

'About a mile up the road,' said Dad, pointing in the right direction, 'you'll see a sharp bend, and it's just there on the left. You can't miss it.'

'I worked in Greenway as a young boy,' said Eamon. 'The

McAllisters always kept it so well. It's great to know a new family are moving in.'

'Maybe the two boys can play together once we get settled,' said Diane hopefully. 'You're very welcome to visit, Peter.'

'*Mummy*,' Simon growled from the back.

'Eh, yes,' said Dad, putting his arm around Peter. 'I'm sure that would be lovely, wouldn't it, Peter?'

Peter looked at Simon's furious face. 'I guess so,' he said, thinking it wouldn't be lovely at all.

* * *

Back at Cooper's Cottage, Maggie had a fine spread waiting for them. Dad and Eamon told Maggie, Kate and Mam about their run-in with the new neighbours.

'Greenway Manor, eh?' remarked Mam, as she poured herself another cup of tea. 'They must have a bob or two to be able to buy that place.'

'Some car, too,' said Dad, helping himself to a bun. 'I wonder what business they're in?'

'Not farming,' laughed Eamon.

Peter nibbled on a piece of rocky road. He had been feeling a little unsettled since meeting the Sinclairs – or one of them anyway. He really hoped he wouldn't have to spend any more time in the company of Simon Sinclair.

The mere thought of it made his tummy flutter. Not the

good flutters that mean something exciting is about to happen, but the ones he got when he was worried. The more he thought about Simon Sinclair, the more his tummy fluttered.

Chapter 2

Operation Plan Bee

'Terrible, just terrible,' Dad tut-tutted over his farming newspaper. He turned the page, shaking his head and mumbling random phrases under his breath. 'Total disaster.' 'Shocking.' 'What are we to do?'

Kate was also reading at the breakfast table. *Animal Monthly* was her favourite magazine. It had pictures and facts about animals in Ireland and all over the world. Kate was already knowledgeable about the sleeping habits of badgers, baboons and brown bears, but lately there was something else that had caught her attention and was making her feel quite cross.

'Is that really true?' she asked no one in particular. 'How awful!' She eagerly turned the pages, shaking her head in disbelief as her eyes scanned the words and pictures.

Peter was too busy 'eating' his porridge to pay much attention to the grumblings of his dad and sister. He hated porridge but had come up with a cunning plan to avoid eating it. He brought each spoonful up to his lips and then quickly moved it under the table to where Blue, his border collie, was waiting

patiently for yet another delicious mouthful. Having a dog who eats everything you hate is pretty useful.

'Mmmmmm, great porridge, Mam,' Peter would occasionally say to deflect his mother's suspicions.

It was late August, which was always a quiet time on the farm. Most of the spring lambs had been sold by now, although Dad had held a few back this year. The market for sheep was so poor, he hoped that if he waited for the later sales the prices would be better. But time was running out, and they had to be sold soon. It was nearly time to put the ram out with the ewes again and get ready for another busy lambing season in the spring.

However, one of the lambs, a young Texel ram, would not be sold and instead would stay at Hazel Tree for breeding. Larry had been the runt of the litter and his mother had rejected him. Dad took him home, and the children helped to bottle-feed him in his early days. He was successfully adopted and had thrived under the care of his new mum. Now Larry was maturing into a fine ram, his emerging physical strength only matched by his strong character and personality.

The future lambs of such a fine purebred Texel ram would no doubt be of high quality and worth a lot of money. The question was ... would it be enough to keep Hazel Tree going over the winter months?

On this morning, Dad's early yard work was done and he

was finishing his 'second breakfast'. He got up so early that a cup of tea and a slice of bread would hold him until the animals had been tended to, then it was home for some eggs, toast and a slice (or two) of bacon.

Mam topped up their tea as Dad continued to read, grunting over the words as he did so. 'I don't know,' he mumbled. 'What are people supposed to do?'

'It's just so unfair,' Kate whimpered from the opposite chair. 'Why isn't someone doing something?'

Mam stood up, holding the teapot in one hand and placing the other squarely on her hip. 'Are you two going to tell me what you're reading, or do I have to guess? Oh, and Peter,' she added, turning his way, 'if I see you giving Blue one more spoonful, you will have porridge for lunch and dinner.'

The gig was up. Peter brought his hand back to the table. Blue, her nose covered with porridge, followed his hand. She hadn't finished that spoonful and a big dollop of porridge fell to the floor.

'I'll just clean that up,' Peter said, moving from his chair to the sink in one quick motion.

'Sheep prices,' said Dad, oblivious to the porridge chaos. 'Things have never been so bad.'

He spun his paper around so Mam could read the headline: *Sheep Prices at an All-Time Low. A Market in Crisis!*

'There's no market at all for us,' Dad said sadly. 'People aren't buying wool, and some supermarkets are stocking imported meat. It's not even local.'

Mam tut-tutted and shook her head. 'Those supermarkets need to remember that without farmers, they would have very little on their shelves.'

'Ahem.' Kate cleared her throat in a bid to get some attention of her own. 'Farmers aren't the only food producers in trouble.'

She looked around to make sure everyone was listening. 'Our bees! Did you know their population is in decline?'

'Good,' said Peter. 'I got stung by a bee once and it hurt.'

Kate glared at him, her eyes growing large. 'First of all, not all bees sting, and if they do it's because they feel threatened. And second, it's the girl bees that have the stinger, so watch out when girls are about.'

'What does *deline* mean, anyway?' Peter asked through a mouthful of horrid porridge.

'*Decline*, Peter,' Kate said again, this time louder. '*Decline* means their population is falling. As in … nearly gone. Like *FOREVERRRRRRR*.'

Her dramatic tone made Peter's forehead crinkle.

'If we don't start protecting bees and their homes, there will be no bees left,' she added, her voice wobbling.

'Ok,' said Peter, wanting to get this conversation over with but not wanting his sister to feel sad. 'What is the big deal if we have no bees?'

'Pollination, of course. They pollinate our plants,' said Kate, rubbing her eyes.

'Eurrrrgh, gross,' said Peter. 'That's what makes all the rivers and lakes dirty.'

Dad chuckled.

'That's *pollution*, Peter,' said Mam with a smile.

'I'm talking about POLLINATION.' Kate was exasperated now. 'Bees carry pollen from one flowering plant to another and pollinate them. Then fruit and berries can grow on our trees and hedges, and our countryside is green and more beautiful. Isn't that right, Dad?'

Kate looked over at her father, who was once more engrossed in his newspaper.

He looked up, baffled by the sudden silence and the three sets of eyes that were on him. 'Eh, yes?' he both asked and answered.

Mam went to the fruit bowl and picked up an apple and a pear. 'Catch!' she shouted, throwing a piece of fruit to Dad and Peter. 'These were flowers before the bees and other pollinators came along. You're right, Kate, it is a problem and I promise we will do something about it.'

Kate beamed. Nobody knew it yet, but she was already planning what she was going to do about it. She had been working on a plan that was so brilliant it made her head spin.

Kate had been stuffing as much bee knowledge into her head as she possibly could, watching documentaries and reading books and magazine articles. She never knew how important bees were – not just for helping us grow fruit and other food, but they also helped habitats to develop which created homes for other animals. Now that Mam was on her side, it was time to put her plan into action. 'Operation Plan Bee' was a go!

Outside the kitchen window, the late-summer sun shone and the melody of farm life played on. Along with the sounds of sheep baa'ing, the new calves bellowed in their low tones. Kate's hens were also part of this special choir, their clucking and scratching becoming so loud that they drowned out the music of the other animals.

Kate's favourite hen, Hettie (aka 'the Boss'), was fussing around the brood that at one point had been her tiny, fluffy chicks. These chicks were now fully grown and laying eggs of their own, which were sold in Maggie and Kate's honesty boxes at the gate of Cooper's Cottage. Fluffing her feathers to show she meant business, Hettie scurried around the group, making sure they stayed together and only pecked at the best worms and bugs.

Once she was happy that they could be left to their own

devices, Hettie made her way to the back door. Her familiar *peck, peck, peck* announced that she was ready to be brought indoors to be with her favourite human.

'Morning, Hettie!' the family chorused, as she hopped into the kitchen. Kate made her way over, enveloping the little hen in a warm embrace.

After the arrival of Hettie's chicks, Maggie and Kate's honesty box empire had grown. They were now known as the 'eggpreneurs', and their one honesty box had become three. People from all over the area came for their eggs, and a queue of cars could often be seen outside Maggie and Eamon's cottage. At one stage, a photographer from the local newspaper had even come to take their photo.

'Right, everyone,' Mam announced as she cleared away the plates from breakfast. 'We have a busy day ahead of us.'

The children looked at each other, worried. Mam's 'busy days' were never fun. This was not good news.

'It's back-to-school shopping!' Mam exclaimed excitedly.

The word 'shopping' was barely out of her mouth when she noticed her two children dashing for the back door. They nearly fell over each other to be the first to escape.

'Freeze!' Mam shouted.

Peter was trying to put his jacket on inside out and Kate was hiding behind Hettie, who was clucking with disapproval. Blue was barking, thinking there was an emergency of some kind, and Dad was laughing into his newspaper.

The words 'back to school' had caused complete panic, and back-to-school shopping was truly the worst kind of shopping.

Peter was desperate. 'Dad, didn't you say something about needing our help for the sheep sales?'

'No, Peter,' said Dad, highly amused. 'Those sales are later this week. We have plenty of time to get ready.'

Now it was Kate's turn. 'I'm pretty sure I have to help Maggie restock the honesty boxes. Those eggs don't find themselves, you know!'

'I've already spoken with Maggie' – Mam's voice sounded dangerous – 'and she is taking care of the boxes today.'

The children knew there was no point in arguing. The most awful day of the summer holidays had arrived, and the new school term was just around the corner.

'We leave in twenty minutes,' Mam said, tapping the face of her watch as Peter and Kate marched out of the room and upstairs to get ready. Once they were gone, Dad lowered his paper again.

'What are we going to do?' he said, looking serious now. 'There's no way we will get decent prices at the sales this week.'

'It will be ok, David,' said Mam softly. 'Things always have a way of working out, you'll see.'

Picking up a tea towel, she threw it straight at him. 'Until then, you can tidy up the breakfast dishes while I get the school uniforms sorted.'

'Aye, aye!' said Dad, saluting his wife like a soldier to his sergeant major.

As the kitchen emptied, Dad re-read the headline: *Sheep Prices at an All-Time Low.*

'I hope you're right, Marian,' he whispered to himself. 'I really hope so.'

Chapter 3

Horsey Ears

'It itches!' Peter moaned as he tugged and wriggled in the jumper that Mam had just pulled over his head. 'And these sleeves are too long,' he said, lifting his arms dramatically.

'You'll grow into it,' Mam exclaimed through gritted teeth.

Meanwhile Kate was pulling at her new elasticated necktie while trying to tell Peter and her mother all about Operation Plan Bee. The fact that they were not really listening annoyed her, so she just spoke louder.

'If everyone kept a space in their gardens for wildflowers and let their grass grow long, well, that would be like Disney-land to bees,' she told them, flapping the end of the tie against her chin as she spoke.

'Kate, it sounds wonderful,' her mother answered, while checking sizes on trousers, 'but can we talk about it later?'

'Why do I have to wear this anyway?' Kate moaned, pulling the tie down as far as it could go.

'Don't stretch it, Kate,' Mam warned.

Suddenly Kate lost her grip and the tie snapped back against

her neck. 'Ouch!' she squealed.

Mam rolled her eyes. She went over and tucked the elastic around the collar of Kate's shirt, then gently rubbed her daughter's reddened neck. 'The sooner you two stop grumbling, the sooner we can leave.'

From his shop counter, Patsy Walsh chuckled. This time of the year was always the same: stressed parents and bored children.

'Oh, hello!' The sound of a friendly voice was in stark contrast to their grumbles.

Mam swung around to see Diane Sinclair standing behind her.

'It's Peter, isn't it?' Diane smiled towards Peter, who quickly pushed up his sleeves to look a bit smarter.

Mam and Kate looked confused.

'Oh, pardon me, we haven't been introduced.' Diane Sinclair extended her hand to Mam. 'I'm Diane Sinclair. We met Peter along with David and Eamon the other day. They were so kind to us when we lost our way on the roads.'

Mam smiled, realising who this smartly dressed lady was. 'Lovely to meet you. I'm Marian Farrelly, and this is Kate.'

Kate smiled shyly at the very elegant lady.

Since their arrival, the Sinclairs had caused quite a stir in Ballynoe. The villagers had been taking turns in guessing their back story, and their theories went from the vaguely possible to the downright ridiculous.

'Heard they're lottery winners,' said Mrs Jones from the butchers.

'Rubbish,' said Mr Thomas, the fishmonger. 'I head they're part of the British royal family. She's 85th in line to the throne.'

'I heard it was 25th,' said Malachy Brennan.

'You're all wrong,' chimed in Mrs Bergin, the local know-it-all. 'I heard they are in the witness protection programme. Mr Sinclair was part of an elite criminal gang.'

The thing was, no one actually knew anything about the Sinclairs, which just added to the mystery (and the rumours).

'It doesn't fit!' Simon Sinclair suddenly appeared behind his mother, tapping the screen of his mobile phone. He was wearing the same school jumper as Peter and Kate.

'This is my son, Simon,' said Diane, tugging at the shoulders of his jumper.

'Ah, you're going to St Brendan's too,' Mam said, with a smile. 'What class are you going into, Simon?'

'Fifth,' Simon answered sharply without looking up.

'Ms Keenan's fifth class,' added Diane quickly.

'Same as Peter,' chipped in Kate.

Peter winced and Simon rolled his eyes.

'You've got to be kidding me,' Simon muttered, throwing a sinister glare in Peter's direction before turning his attention back to the screen.

'How lovely, you will be in the same class!' Diane said, trying to distract from her son's bad manners. She took the phone from him and pointed at the large table of jumpers in the middle of the shop floor.

'Hey, I was using that!' he snapped at his mother.

'Go find a bigger size in that jumper,' came Diane's stern reply.

Mam turned to Peter and Kate. 'You two can go and change. I think we've had enough shopping for one day.'

When all the children were gone, Diane turned to Mam, and her smile faded. 'I apologise for Simon,' she said, looking stressed. 'This move has not been easy for him, and I suppose it doesn't help with his father being away so much.'

From their changing rooms, Peter and Kate listened through the curtains. Were they going to find out more about the mysterious Sinclairs?

'We've always wanted to move back to the countryside,' Diane continued. 'Both myself and my husband Derek grew up on farms, and we wanted our son to enjoy the same kind of happy childhood we had.'

Mam put her hand on Diane's shoulder, sensing that she needed someone to talk to.

'We thought giving him his own phone would help with the move. He could keep in touch with his friends, call his dad whenever he wanted. But now that phone is all he looks at.'

'These things take time,' Mam said, trying to sound reassuring. 'It's a big change for him, but he will come to love it here, you'll see.'

'Thank you … Marian.' Diane's face brightened. 'I do hope so.'

Peter emerged from the dressing room, handing his mother the crumpled-up uniform they were about to buy.

'Peter, those calves in your front field are very impressive,' said Diane, back to her sunny self. 'Angus breed, am I right?'

'Eh, yes.' Peter was impressed. He hadn't thought someone like Diane Sinclair would know anything about farming, let alone breeds of cattle.

'I thought so! My father was a beef farmer, and I always knew my Simmental from my Friesian and my Limousin from my Charolais.'

'They all seem stupid to me.' Simon was also back. Clutching a new jumper in one hand, he stretched the other hand out, waiting to be reunited with his phone.

'And what kind of work are you in?' Mam spotted an opportunity to change the subject and get the inside scoop on the Sinclairs. 'Still farming in some way?'

'Oh, I wish,' said Diane with a faraway look in her eye. 'My husband and I set up a small TV production company some time ago, and that has kept us very busy.'

'A production company?' Mam looked confused. 'I'm sorry,

I don't understand.'

'We make TV programmes,' said Diane. 'Mostly documentaries and children's programmes, which we broadcast through the SoFun Network.'

'OH MY GOD!' Kate threw back the curtains of the changing room dramatically and stood there, open mouthed. 'You're the Sinclairs who own the SoFun Network? You make *All About Bugs*? And *Horse Sense*? And *Zoo Times*?'

Diane laughed. 'Why, yes! I do hope you enjoy them. We have a special passion for animal shows.'

'They are my favourite!' Kate's eyes were as wide as saucers. 'I must have watched them all a million times, they are ...'

'Boring.' Simon finished Kate's sentence. 'Totally boring.'

Kate glared at Simon. 'No, they're not!' she retorted, shuffling past him. 'Thanks to *Horse Sense*, I learned all about how horses speak with their ears.' She put her hands on either side of her head as if they were horses' ears and moved them in line with her actions. 'Point forward for alert, back for angry, and to the side for sleepy.'

Diane was delighted and applauded the little girl. 'Bravo Kate! You must give me a tour of that farm of yours. I hear great things about your hen eggs.'

'Actually,' said Mam, 'why don't you take my number?' Mam called out her mobile number to Diane, who saved it to her phone.

'Well, it's official,' said Diane. 'We are neighbours now!'

The two women smiled warmly at each other and said their goodbyes.

As Mam paid for the uniforms, she glanced back at Diane and Simon. She could tell that Simon was getting a stern talking to. Diane looked flushed, throwing her arms in the air while an indifferent Simon stared up at the ceiling.

Peter watched too. Now he was in the same class as Simon as well as neighbours. It was going to be hard to avoid him. Peter's tummy started to flutter once again.

Back-to-school shopping *and* bumping into Simon Sinclair? *Worst day ever*, Peter thought, shaking his head.

Kate, though, was feeling very excited. How amazing that the makers of her favourite TV shows were her new neighbours! And in no time Mam and Diane would be BFFs. *Best day ever*, she thought dreamily.

* * *

Back at Hazel Tree, Dad met them at the front door. 'I've got some news!' he said, a big smile spreading across his face.

'Oh, is it that the Sinclairs are hugely successful TV producers and make loads of really popular TV shows?' Kate said, floating past him with a big grin of her own.

'How did you know?' Dad sounded crushed. Kate had totally stolen his thunder.

'We have our sources,' said Mam, laughing. 'But how did you know?'

'Well, Mandy Bergin heard it from Danny Thomas while she was buying her kippers, and he heard it from Sally Jones who was packing her window with rump roast, and she heard it from ...'

'Patsy Walsh in the clothes shop?' finished Mam. 'I thought I saw him listening in when I was speaking with Diane Sinclair.'

'You were talking to her?' Now Dad was intrigued.

'Such a lovely lady,' said Mam, waiting for Peter and Kate to be out of earshot before continuing. 'She has her hands full with that Simon though.'

Mam told Dad all about her conversation with Diane and her worries about Simon. How the Sinclairs had grown up on farms and how they hoped a country setting would be good for their son.

'Maybe that's just what he needs,' said Dad. 'A few days on a farm with a shovel and a fork. It would do him the world of good.'

'You know ... That's not a bad idea,' said Mam. 'He can spend a day up here with us. He and Peter can get to know each other before school starts.'

Peter and Kate, who were secretly listening at the top of the stairs, looked at each other in horror. A day with Simon Sinclair? How on earth were they going to get out of this one?

'He's the worrrrrst,' groaned Kate. 'How can Mam and Dad do this to us?'

'Do this to *us*?' Peter replied. 'You mean *me*! I'm the one who has to spend the day with him and go to school with him.'

'I'm sorry, Peter,' Kate said with some sympathy, before quickly adding, 'Why don't you help me with my new Operation Plan Bee flyers? You're way better at art than I am.'

Peter's head dropped and he turned his back on his sister. 'You only care about your stupid bee thing,' he snapped.

Kate didn't know what to say as her brother marched angrily to his room. He slammed the door behind him, making the windows rattle.

'Stop slamming doors!' Mam called from downstairs. 'Those windows are here longer than any of us, you know.'

Kate went into her bedroom, where a whole wall was crammed with bee pictures and pollination diagrams. Operation Plan Bee was taking over! She opened her sketch pad and looked at the plans for her own bee garden. It was going to look so wonderful, and she had just the right spot for it!

At the back door, where the concrete surface came to an end, there was a patch of grass that got all the morning sun. Kate had often seen wildflowers such as dandelions, daisies and buttercups bloom there, and those were a perfect natural food source for hungry bees.

For added colour, Kate wanted to plant some wildflowers of her own, and she wrote down a list of her favourite ones:

lavender, oxeye daisy, poppies and crocuses. The whole area would be a pollinator's heaven.

She would need something large to plant the seeds in … Eamon or Dad should have just the thing, like maybe an old bucket or barrel that was no longer needed on the farm. She tapped her lip with her colouring pencil. She was also planning to ask them for help planting the seeds.

Kate glanced down at her flyer – she was so proud of it. She had drawn the bee herself and was going to use some of her honesty box money to get a hundred copies printed. If a hundred people read her flyer and created their own pollinator's heaven, these bee gardens could be all over Ballynoe … and all over the county … and maybe even nationwide!

I hope a hundred will be enough, she thought to herself. Her stomach fluttered with excitement.

Operation Plan Bee
We need your help!

*   ★   Plant more flowers – bees like their nectar
*   ★   Grow more herbs – they help make our food nicer too
*   ★   Don't mow your lawn so much – dandelions aren't that bad!
*   ★   Build a bee hotel – so bees can 'hum' and stay a while

Bee nice to us!

* * *

'Hello, Diane. It's Marian Farrelly here.'

From his room, Peter could hear his mother. Her telephone voice was always so loud.

'No, it's no problem at all,' his mother was saying. 'I can collect him.'

Another pause. 'Say about noon? Great, see you then!'

He heard her click off the phone and groaned.

That was that then. Simon Sinclair was coming over, and there was nothing Peter could do about it. Even though they had barely spoken, it didn't take a genius to see that Simon was not someone Peter would be friends with. They had nothing in common, and he was snooty, rude and constantly cross.

The sinking feeling in his stomach made Peter's eyes sting with tears. Tomorrow was going to be awful.

He heard the door creak, and he looked up. Blue's nose pushed the door and her head popped around.

Peter smiled. 'At least I have you,' he said to his best pal.

Sensing her master's sadness, Blue barged through the door and jumped straight up onto the bed. She nuzzled Peter's neck before pushing him down and drowning him in licks.

'Ah, Blue,' Peter giggled, hugging her tightly and putting his tear-stained face into her soft fur.

Meanwhile, over in Greenway, another boy was in his room feeling sad. Simon Sinclair looked at the messages on his BackChat App. Each alert from his friends lit up his phone and darkened his mood.

```
THAT FOOTBALL CAMP WAS THE BEST
MY MUM ALREADY SIGNED ME UP FOR NEXT YEAR
HAVING A PIZZA PARTY LATER - WHO'S COMING
MAKE SURE YOU GET EXTRA PEPPERONI
SORRY YOU WON'T BE THERE SIMON
```

Their words made him feel cross. He wasn't cross at them – he was cross at his parents. This was all their fault. His real friends were hundreds of miles away, having so much fun. So much fun without him. Because he was stuck here, in this place, with no one.

Chapter 4

Greenway Manor

Click whirr, click whirr, click whirr ... The sound of the photocopier behind the counter at Bedford's Business & School Supplies was hypnotic. Kate's eyes scanned right to left as she watched her Operation Plan Bee flyers fill up the tray.

'Seventy-six, seventy-seven, seventy-eight ...' she counted as they went through.

'I don't need a counter on the machine with you!' said Eoin Bedford, laughing.

Bedford's was always a flurry of activity at this time of year.

Eoin was glad to help Kate with her copies, as packing shelves with schoolbooks, pencil cases and pens could get a bit dull. He worked in his parents' shop every summer and had known Kate and Peter since they were little.

'Come and see for yourself,' said Eoin, raising the hinged part of the countertop. 'You can even tell me if we're running low on paper.'

Kate's eyes grew wide with excitement. 'I can go behind

the counter?' she squealed with delight. 'It'll be like I'm in charge!'

'Well, not exactly.' Eoin sounded a bit worried now. 'More like … a helper.'

That was good enough for Kate. She proudly walked through to take up her new position.

Eoin picked up a flyer. 'Operation Plan Bee,' he read aloud. 'What's all this about?'

Excited to talk about her utterly brilliant plan again, Kate launched into a full presentation of how the bees were in trouble and how we can all make a difference by following her Operation Plan Bee.

He's going to regret asking her that, thought Mam, chuckling to herself. She turned her attention back to Peter. After the torture of uniform shopping, she hoped that getting school stationery would be a little easier.

'Is it pens or pencils?' she asked.

Peter shrugged his shoulders. 'Dunno,' came the reply as he walked by the shelves.

'Copybooks or hard-back journals?'

'Dunno,' came the reply once again.

'Peter, be helpful.' Mam was growing exasperated now. 'You have the list, read it.'

Sighing aloud, Peter started reading. 'Pens, journals, rulers, pencils, rubbers, sharpeners and a folder …'

With ninja-like skills, Mam swooped and gathered the items as Peter rattled them out. 'Done!' she said proudly and headed to the cash desk.

Peter followed behind, deep in thought. He was worried about the day ahead with Simon. What were they going to do? What were they going to talk about? Was Simon going to be mean all day or just some of it?

He decided to try one more time. 'Please, Mam. Please call off Simon's visit. Tell them I'm sick, pleeeeaaaassssee.'

Mam took a deep breath. Putting the school supplies on the counter, she spoke slowly to Peter. 'That poor boy has had to say goodbye to all his friends and his home. The least we can do is be friendly and help him to settle in. How would you feel if it was you?'

Tears stung Peter's eyes. Could the grownups not see how utterly rotten Simon Sinclair was?

'Will that be all?' Eoin asked as he started scanning their items. He looked over at Peter and smiled. 'How's that dog of yours? What's her name … Red? Purple? Yellow?'

'Blue,' whispered Peter, smiling at Eoin's joke. 'It's Blue, and she's good, thank you.'

'Best sheepdog I've seen for some time,' said Eoin, putting their purchases into a bag. 'Are you off to the sheep sales this week?'

'Yes, we're getting the last of the spring stock ready today,' said Mam. 'Fingers crossed they'll do better than the last ones.'

'It's not good at the moment, is it?' Eoin sounded sorry.

'That's farming for you,' said Mam. 'It's always up and down.'

'We got some new calves,' Kate piped up from behind the counter. She had stuck a pencil behind her ear, thinking it made her look more professional. 'Angus heifers.'

'Fantastic,' said Eoin. 'I'm going to agricultural college in October. You guys might be able to teach me a thing or two!'

Peter smiled. He liked Eoin. He always gave them stickers and lollipops when they went into the shop. It would be fun to have him visit Hazel Tree.

Eoin reached over and took a flyer from the top of Kate's bundle. 'How about I stick this one here at the counter? We get so many customers at this time of year, it will be great exposure for your Plan Bee.'

'Operation Plan Bee,' Kate corrected him, 'and yes please.' She jumped up and down, dropping some pages as she did so.

Eoin picked a small box with a lid from a shelf behind him. 'Here, put them into this,' he said, taking the flyers and carefully placing them in the box. 'We don't want them blowing away. Otherwise your Operation Plan Bee will be Operation Litterbug.'

After happily taking a lollipop from Eoin, the children said their goodbyes and headed for the car. It was time to go to Greenway Manor.

* * *

Mam swung the car into the large cobbled entrance and stopped in front of Greenway Manor's imposing black iron gates. As she hopped out to ring the buzzer, Peter and Kate took in their surroundings, their mouths wide open.

Perfectly trimmed box hedging ran along the bottom of curved limestone walls. Small cone-shaped pillars ran in front of the hedging, with heavy chains hanging ornately in between each cone.

'It's like something out of a movie,' whispered Kate.

Within the walls were lush flower beds, and even though the season was coming to an end, lavender plants stood high among the dusty pink heathers and bright marigolds. Kate smiled as she watched the bees dancing from flower head to flower head.

A low whirring noise could be heard as the gates slowly came to life. Mam got back into the car and as they passed through the gates, it was like they were entering a whole new world.

Peter couldn't be sure, but it felt like Mam was driving a little bit slower than normal, her head turning from side to side as she drank in the views.

Stud fencing ran along the avenue, with large and rather overgrown paddocks behind. Majestic chestnut trees were dotted around the fields, their leaves, like an umbrella, casting shade over the ground below.

Soon the avenue opened up to reveal its finest jewel.

'Whooooooo …' The three voices were in unison as Greenway Manor came into view.

Standing over three floors, it was without a doubt the biggest house the children had ever seen. The wings on either side curved gently inwards, as if they were two hands protecting the main building. Through the enormous bay windows on the ground floor, there was the tiniest glimpse of chandeliers behind the long drapes, which flowed elegantly down.

Mam pulled up in front of a circular rose bed, and before they were even out of the car, one half of the arched front doors swung open and Diane Sinclair stepped forward. She waved happily.

'You are so very welcome,' she said, smiling warmly as Mam and the children climbed the granite steps.

'Your house is beautiful, Diane,' Mam said as they reached the top.

'Oh, stop it,' said Diane, with a wave of her hand. 'It's a house second and a home first. Why don't you come in for a cup of coffee? Simon is still getting himself together.'

* * *

He watched their arrival from his upstairs bedroom window before slumping back onto his bed. A whole day with that

Peter and his annoying little sister.

'Eurrgh, it's not fair,' Simon groaned to himself.

Ping!

The sound of (yet another) alert on his mobile phone. He reached for it and tapped the screen.

It was a picture. Simon clicked it open, using his fingers to grow and stretch the image across his screen.

All his friends laughing and joking at the pizza party the night before. They looked so happy. Simon threw the phone back down and curled up on his bed.

'I hate it here!' he shouted into his pillow, fighting back tears.

* * *

Diane ushered Peter, Kate and Mam indoors. Stepping into the hallway, they cast their eyes over the massive staircase that split at the landing, one flight going left and one going right. Large paintings and tapestries hung all around the walls, and a huge chandelier threw rainbow dots on the cream marbled tiles at their feet.

They followed Diane through a sitting room and a huge dining room. Kate tried to count how many chairs there were but only got to ten before they had passed through to the next room.

'This place is nicer than a hotel,' she whispered to Peter.

'These guys are loaded.'

Peter nodded. The Sinclairs were so lucky. Simon should have been the happiest person in the world.

They entered a large, open-plan kitchen, where the smell of freshly brewed coffee filled their nostrils – as did the aroma of warm cookies.

'Help yourselves, you two,' said Diane, sliding the plate of cookies towards them. They glanced at Mam and on her subtle nod of approval, they dug in.

'Mmmmmm,' mumbled Peter. 'They're all warm and the chocolate chips are melting.'

'Oh, I am glad you like them,' said Diane, laughing. 'The internet is so patchy, I've resorted to using my mother's old cookbooks and whatever I can remember.'

'You really shouldn't have gone to all this trouble,' said Mam as a cup of steaming hot coffee appeared in front of her.

'It really is no bother,' said Diane, pouring herself one. 'I was looking forward to the company, if I'm to be honest.'

Glancing over at the door, Diane sighed. 'What is Simon up to? Maybe you two could go find him, and us mums can have a chat.'

Sliding off their stools, Peter and Kate headed back down the way they came. The sound of their mother's voice faded as they got further from her.

'Eleven, twelve, thirteen ...' Kate picked up her chair-counting where she had left off. 'Twenty, twenty-one, twenty-two ... Twenty-two people can sit at that table, Peter!'

But Peter wasn't really listening to his sister. He was trying to figure out where Simon might be.

'Simon?' he called out gingerly. 'It's Peter and Kate. Your mam told us to come look for you.'

After a brief silence, a snarl rang out from somewhere upstairs. 'I'll be down in a minute,' Simon growled.

Peter and Kate glanced at each other as some loud thumping told them Simon was indeed on his way. They looked up to see him coming down the first flight of steps, thumping each one as if his foot were a fist.

Just then, Diane appeared in the hallway. 'Simon, there you are. Why don't you take Peter and Kate for a tour outside? We're just finishing our coffees.'

Simon threw his mother a disgruntled look. 'Come on,' he said through gritted teeth.

The children followed behind.

'You have a lovely house,' Peter said, trying to sound friendly.

'It's massive! How many rooms are there? Why do you need a table for twenty-two people? Are your parents loaded?' Kate's questions came thick and fast.

Peter looked over to his sister, gesturing for her to be quiet. Kate shrugged her shoulders. There was so much she wanted to know.

Simon said nothing and just stomped out the front door and left towards the far wing of the house. Through the windows, Peter and Kate saw a room with a snooker table, a massive TV screen and a projector. Two gaming chairs were set up in front of the screen. The headsets were clipped onto the sides with the game controllers underneath.

'Is that a games room?' asked Peter.

'What? No way!' exclaimed Kate as she ran over for a closer look. 'A whole room just for games?' She pressed her face and hands up against the window.

'Get back!' shouted Simon. 'You're dirtying the glass.'

Kate stood back, a little embarrassed. 'I was only trying to get a closer look,' she said quietly.

'Only my friends are allowed in there,' Simon spat out as he marched on ahead.

Kate and Peter followed a couple of paces behind.

'He has friends?' Kate whispered to her brother, who looked more worried now than ever.

To the rear of Greenway Manor were large lawns and yet more gardens and flower beds. A gravelled path, dotted with statues, led the way to a large lake with a long wooden jetty. The children spotted a small boat tied to the side. In the middle of the lake was an island, where a cabin stood just beyond the water's edge.

'Does someone live out there?' asked Kate.

'No,' said Simon, sounding irritated. 'Me and my dad stay there when we go fishing on the lake.'

'Cool,' said Kate. 'Where is your dad?'

'He's not here,' Simon snarled. 'He's busy working.'

'Then when do you go fishing?' asked Kate.

Peter threw her another 'be quiet' look, while Simon just glared and said nothing.

As they walked past the lake, they came to an older part of the estate with large sheds and stone outhouses.

'What's this place then?' asked Kate.

'It used to be the farmyard,' said Simon. 'There's nothing here.'

As they crossed the overgrown cobbles of what must have been a wonderful farmyard once upon a time, Peter was drawn to a path that ran to the rear of the old sheds.

'Where does that go?' he asked Simon. Without waiting for an answer, he started to follow the path.

'Hey, you can't go there!' Simon hissed.

Behind the old farmyard of Greenway Manor was a vast wooded area. Old gnarled trees reached out of the ground, climbing high above the children's heads.

Nestled between the trees and dense scrub was a structure not created by nature. The long stony path led Peter to the arched entrance to what looked like an old passageway.

'Woowwww,' said Kate, appearing at Peter's side. 'Where

does that go?'

The children moved in for a closer look. Kate, suddenly feeling scared, grabbed the back of Peter's jumper.

At the entrance was a stone floor with deep grooves running from side to side. The floor sloped gently downwards before running on into the darkness.

'What are those lines for?' Kate whispered, her voice echoing through the tunnel.

'So animals don't slip on the hard ground,' said Peter. 'It's the same on the old sheds in our yard at Hazel Tree.'

'Are there animals in there?' asked Kate, alarmed at the thought.

'I doubt it,' said Peter. 'Not anymore.'

The outer stone walls of the tunnel were covered with a blanket of thick green moss, and over time ivy and weeds had fallen over the entrance, doing their best to conceal the darkened passage that lay beyond.

'You two shouldn't be here!' said Simon, coming up from behind. 'Come on, time we got back.'

'But what is this place?' Peter was now the one full of questions. 'Where does it go?'

'It's none of your business,' came the cutting reply.

As they followed Simon back along the old path, Peter noticed a large pile of ivy and briars lying to one side of the tunnel's entrance. They must have been pulled off, as the stone underneath looked cleaner and less weathered than the rest. Someone had been here, and recently too.

'Peter! Kate!' Mam's voice rang out across the garden. 'It's time to go!'

The children made their way back to the front door of Greenway, where Mam and Diane were waiting for them.

Diane handed Simon a jacket, which he snatched from her. He clambered into the back seat of Mam's car, the sound of the seat belt clicking into position the only noise to be heard.

His mother was still standing at the door as they drove down the avenue. As they reached the iron gates, they glided open, allowing the travellers to pass through.

'So cool,' whispered Kate.

Simon looked over at her and for the briefest of moments, Peter thought he saw a glimmer of a smile.

His own thoughts went back to the darkened tunnel. It looked like a passageway. But to where? How far did it go, and how long had it been there? Something told him that Simon Sinclair knew the answers to these questions. But was he willing to answer them?

Chapter 5

You'll Need Some Wellies

The drive to Hazel Tree from Greenway Manor took mere moments. The car had barely stopped and Kate already had her seatbelt off. Clutching her box of flyers, she couldn't wait to get started on the next phase of Operation Plan Bee.

She was going to set up her bee garden before heading to the honesty box at the gate of Cooper's Cottage to hand out flyers. It was always busy in the early evenings, as people driving home from work were looking to get some fresh free-range eggs for their tea.

Eamon and Dad had agreed to help her with the planting, digging and sowing. Eamon had the compost ready, and Dad had bought her some seeds in the local farm shop.

As Mam took the bags of stationery from the boot of the car, Kate turned to Simon and Peter. 'Do you two want to help with my bee garden?' she asked hopefully.

Simon laughed and rolled his eyes. 'Eh, no!' *Why would I want to hang around with the little sister and her boring bees*, he thought.

Shrugging her shoulders, Kate headed for the house, leaving the boys behind.

'Right, you two,' said Mam. 'Peter, you show Simon around. I know Dad and Eamon need some help getting the sheep ready for the sales, and those calves need to be fed.'

Mam watched them as they skulked off. *That'll keep them busy until dinner*, she thought.

Putting the shopping bags down, she reached for her phone. She should let Dad know the boys were on their way – the kids weren't allowed on the farm unless the adults knew to expect them.

As Simon walked behind Peter, he suddenly grabbed his nose dramatically. 'Eurrrrgh! What's that smell? I think I'm going to be sick!'

'What smell?' Peter asked. 'I can't smell anything.'

'How can you not smell that?' Simon said, pretending to retch. 'It's positively putrid.'

Peter sniffed the air. 'There's no smell except a farm smell,' he answered, before walking off.

Simon followed, both hands over his nose.

They walked the path from the house to the main yard. The sheds were just a few yards from the back door, and beyond the buildings lay the fields and paddocks.

Simon took in his surroundings, lowering his hands as he did so, momentarily forgetting about the 'smell'. He watched Peter lift the latch on one of the old sheds and pick up two buckets.

'Here, you can hold this,' he said, handing a bucket to Simon. Peter then picked up a scoop and opened a bag filled with small brown pellets.

'What's that?' Simon asked, trying not to sound too interested.

'Calf nuts,' said Peter. He placed two scoops of nuts into each bucket before moving to another bag that lay behind.

'What are you doing now?'

'I need to mix those nuts with some of this calf crunch,' answered Peter.

Suddenly a small mouse jumped out of the meal bag and ran towards the open door, where Simon was standing with his bucket of nuts.

'Arrrrrrrgh!' Simon screamed, throwing the bucket at the scarpering mouse. 'Vermin! How disgusting! Those things are full of diseases.'

Peter shook his head and walked over. Using his hands, he scooped up the pile of fallen nuts and refilled the bucket. He handed it back to an obviously shaken Simon.

'Mice have to eat too,' Peter said, trying to hide his smile.

It was funny to see the hoity-toity Simon Sinclair afraid of a tiny mouse. Maybe he wasn't as tough as he thought he was.

The calves could hear the buckets being filled and were trotting over to their feeders, mooing loudly, their long grey tongues licking their nostrils.

'Ugh, gross,' muttered Simon, retching a little.

Peter opened the gate. Simon paused but Peter beckoned him to enter the field.

The two feeders stood low to the ground and had a narrow metal tray that was at least two metres long.

'Start at the far end,' instructed Peter, 'and pour the nuts along the tray.'

Simon watched as Peter, with great skill, tipped his bucket so the contents gently spilled, lining the tray with the brown pellets. The gathered calves ran to their places along the feeder and quietly munched away.

Suddenly Simon felt something push against him. He looked down to see three calves nudging his bucket. Another one was sucking at the corner of his jacket.

'Hey!' he cried out. 'Get away, you'll ruin my jacket!'

The calf stopped and looked up at him with her big brown eyes. She wore yellow tags with the number 1360 in each ear. Simon smiled and lifted his hand towards her.

He was within touching distance of 1360 when suddenly a bolder calf, impatient for her grub, headbutted the bucket and knocked it from his hand. The sudden movement spooked 1360, who bolted away.

The bucket and its contents were, once more, all over the ground. Five unfed calves ran towards the pile of nuts and crunch, shoving Simon out of the way and straight into a big pile of …

SQUEEEALCCCCCCHHHHHHHH!

'Bleurrrrrgh!' Simon's face crumpled as his spotlessly clean designer runners were submerged in a large pile of cow poo.

He glared over at Peter, who was already picking up the dropped bucket and trying hard not to smile. It seemed like Simon Sinclair might not be cut out for life on the farm.

'What on earth are you two at?' Eamon appeared at the gate, scratching his head at the sight before him. 'Did no one tell you about the luxury of a good pair of wellies when visiting a farm, Mr Sinclair?'

'No,' was Simon's curt reply.

Eamon opened the gate and went to Simon's aid. He reached out his hand. Simon recoiled when he saw the grime and dirt on Eamon's hand.

'Don't worry,' Eamon laughed. 'It's clean dirt. I was helping Kate sow some seeds for her bee garden.'

Reluctantly, Simon took a hold. Eamon's strength surprised him, and a loud *SHHLURRRPP* noise could be heard as his foot was pulled to freedom.

By now the calves had finished their meal. Some gathered around the trio, mooing for more food, while the timid ones kept their distance. 1360 pushed her way forward, once again making a beeline for Simon.

'It seems you have a friend,' Eamon remarked in a low voice as the calf nuzzled Simon and began to lick and suck his jacket again.

'Can I touch it?' Simon asked quietly.

'Yes,' said Eamon. 'Lift your hand slowly and just say "suck, suck".'

Taking a deep breath, Simon reached out his hand to the little heifer. He paused and looked to Eamon for reassurance. Eamon mouthed the words 'suck, suck'.

'Suck, suck,' Simon whispered to the curious animal.

1360 moved her nostrils towards the outstretched hand.

'That's it, lad,' whispered Eamon. 'Keep your hand still. Let her come to you.'

1360 sniffed and licked the tips of Simon's fingers. Her long grey tongue felt like sandpaper on his skin.

Wincing at first, Simon suddenly broke into a big smile. He lifted his hand and stroked the hair along 1360's nose. As he gently scratched her forehead, she dropped her head and moved in closer.

'That's the way,' laughed Eamon. 'Look at how much she is enjoying that. You're a natural.'

As the rest of the calves moved away, 1360 followed them. Simon looked on, still smiling. 'What are those in her ears?' he asked.

'That's her special number tag,' said Eamon. 'It tells us everything about that little heifer, such as where and when she was born. You'll see a lot of farm animals with those ear tags.'

Back in the main yard, Eamon brought Simon to a water tap where he could wash the cow poo from his shoes.

Eamon walked back over to Peter, who was grinning at the memory of Simon's perfect runners stuck in the sloppy poop pie.

'Now, Peter,' Eamon gently scolded, 'we can't all be experts at our first try. We have our work cut out with that one, but we'll win him round, you'll see.'

'How?' asked Peter. 'He doesn't even like us, and he certainly doesn't want to be here.'

'I think he does,' said Eamon, winking. 'He just doesn't know it yet.'

Gathering up the buckets, they all headed back to the yard. There was important work to be done, and all hands were needed.

The last of the spring lambs were due to go to the sales mart the following morning. It was going to be an early start. Dad was rounding them up in the meadow and moving them to a shed where they would stay overnight. This would save time when loading them into the trailer the next day.

As they approached the meadow, Blue came bounding up to Peter, whimpering and wagging her tail at the joy of seeing her young master.

'Where have you lot been?' Dad shouted from the field. 'Come on, Peter. Eamon and Simon, you get the gate ready.'

Peter let out a shrill whistle to tell Blue it was time for work. They made their way to the centre of the field, and Peter gave his first command: 'Away to me.'

Like lightning, Blue circled right around the sheep, herding them towards the gate.

'Grab this, Simon!' shouted Eamon, throwing him a long rope with a clip at the end. He clipped his own end to the gate at the meadow.

'Run your end to the shed,' shouted Eamon, pointing to the building close by. 'Clip it to the metal ring on the wall, then come back to me.'

Spurred into action, Simon ran as instructed. He was not accustomed to hearing so many orders at once and found himself both giddy and flustered. There was something about Eamon that he liked, and he didn't want to let him down.

With both ends of the rope in place, they had created a makeshift passage for the sheep to follow. Simon watched in amazement as Peter and Blue skilfully moved the sheep into position.

Blue crouched low, moving only to guide the flock to the gate where Eamon and Simon were waiting. Their job was simple but crucial: they had to make sure the sheep followed along the rope towards the shed. If the sheep veered left, they would be heading to the far end of the laneway and towards the main road. Dad had blocked off the laneway with his tractor, but sheep are good at wiggling through even the smallest of gaps. No matter how good their plan was, all it would take would be one skittish sheep to set panic in the flock and create disaster.

Dad made his way to the shed to check that the doors were open wide to welcome in these new arrivals. 'Ready!' he called out to the rest of team.

Blue looked to Peter, awaiting the command.

Simon looked on in amazement. 'How does she know what to do?' he whispered to Eamon.

'Because they're a team,' said Eamon.

Simon looked confused.

Eamon explained how Blue had been a late bloomer as a sheepdog. When she was young, she didn't listen to commands and would bite and nip the ewes instead of herding them in. In fact, Eamon had pretty much given up hope for the young collie until the night of the vixen attack.

'She proved herself when we needed her most,' Eamon told Simon. 'Had it not been for Blue, we would have lost many of the sheep you see here.'

The sound of Peter's whistle brought them back to attention.

The small flock were at the gate of the meadow. They needed to stay right and be herded towards Dad, who was waiting at the open shed.

'As they move in,' explained Eamon, 'we'll stay alongside them to stop them moving out of our passage. Blue and Peter will manage the back.'

As the first sheep entered the roped-off passage, it hesitated, looking right and then left. It suddenly jerked left and went to bolt under the rope, a move that would no doubt make the others follow.

'Quick, Simon,' shouted Eamon, 'block her!'

Using instincts he didn't know he had, Simon turned sharp, skidding in the mud as he did so. He spread his arms low and wide, ushering the animal back and turning it in the right direction. The other sheep quickly followed.

Blue ran to the outside to make sure no others tried the same move. She inspected each sheep as it moved past her. She then tucked in behind the last one, moving them all forward.

Eamon and Simon walked beside the flock, their arms spread wide. Peter pulled the gate and caught up with Blue in managing the rear.

As the last sheep entered the shed, Dad slid the door shut and bolted it.

'Great work, everyone!' cried Dad. 'We'll make a shepherd out of you yet, Simon.'

'I think he needs a pair of wellies first,' laughed Eamon.

Simon looked down at his shoes. They were well and truly in an awful state by now, but for some strange reason, he didn't feel cross. Instead, he felt happy – happy and proud of what they had just achieved.

He smiled back at Eamon and shrugged his shoulders, showing how his filthy runners didn't matter. Then he looked over at Peter and his dad.

'That was great work, son,' Dad said, hugging Peter tightly. 'You and Blue really are a great team.'

Suddenly the familiar feeling of anger returned, and Simon's new-found happiness was no more.

Perfect, thought Kate. *It's perfect.*

It had been a busy afternoon all round, and Kate was nearly finished getting her bee garden set up.

Eamon had found her a great planter. Once used as a drinker for the sheep, it was a large plastic barrel sliced down the middle. He placed it to the side of the small green area, resting it against two granite blocks to stop it from falling forward. Eamon had filled the planter with compost and showed Kate how to sow wildflower seeds.

Using his finger, Eamon dug a straight line, or drill, in the dark-brown compost. *I wonder if this is how gardeners get 'green fingers'*, Kate thought to herself.

She copied Eamon, enjoying the earthy smell of the compost on her hands. When they had five of these little trenches dug, Kate (under Eamon's watchful eye) gently poured a thin line of seeds along each.

At the end of each drill, Kate stuck the empty seed packet to the front so she knew which flowers would grow there. She had chosen flowers that would bloom all year round, so the honeybees – who don't hibernate – would have lots of lovely food to store in their hives no matter the season.

As Eamon left to move the ewes, Kate was busy covering over each drill, sprinkling enough water to encourage these little seeds to grow.

She and Eamon had decided to leave the grassy area next to the planter as it was. Even though the grass was quite short now, it would grow in no time. The bees would have shelter, and native wildflowers such as clover, dandelions and daisies could grow freely. It really was going to be a heavenly sanctuary for her bees. Kate couldn't wait.

Standing back to admire her work, she checked her watch. Just enough time to hand out some flyers at the honesty boxes.

GRRRUUMBLE!

But Kate's tummy had other plans. She had been so consumed by her garden she had nearly missed the dinner call, and she was absolutely starving!

'I want all hands washed!' Mam was belting out the orders to Peter and Simon when Kate entered the kitchen. Looking down at her own hands, Kate joined the 'wash' line too, knowing that she wasn't going to get away with it.

The smell of Mam's stew made Kate's tummy grumble even more as she made her way from the sink to the table. The only sounds that could be heard after that were the clinking of forks on plates and the swishing of juice in glasses.

It was some time before Simon came up for air. He looked down at his plate and couldn't believe how much he had eaten. He was hungrier than he thought – in fact, hungrier than he had been for a long time.

He glanced over at Peter and Kate, both tucking in and not paying him too much attention. Still, it felt nice to be here, to feel needed.

'Just look at the state of these. What will your mother say?' Mam was busy scrubbing the now hardened poo and mud from Simon's shoes.

Forgetting he had no shoes on, Simon curled his stocking feet underneath his chair, suddenly feeling a little embarrassed. 'She won't care,' he replied. 'I can always get a new pair.'

'A new pair?' Peter looked up suddenly. 'Because they got dirty?'

Simon threw Peter a withering look, which sent him scurrying back to his plate in silence.

'Nonsense,' said Mam. 'They'll be as good as new by the time I'm done.'

Kate was finished first and she jumped up, startling Blue and Hettie as she did so. There wasn't a moment to lose. It was nearly five o'clock – rush hour at the honesty boxes was about to start.

'What's the hurry?' Mam asked Kate's back as she bolted for the door.

'I have to be ready with my flyers,' Kate cried out. 'I can't miss my chance!'

'Well, hang on,' called Mam, and Kate paused at the door. 'You won't be giving a good impression with gravy on your face.'

Grabbing some kitchen towel and running it under the tap, Mam cleaned a grinning Kate before kissing her lightly on top of her head.

'Maaaaam …' groaned Kate.

'I can't help it,' said Mam. 'I am very proud of you and all the work you are doing.'

The grin returned to Kate's slightly blushing face, and she skipped from the room, grabbing her flyers as she did so.

As Mam turned back to the sink, she saw Simon watching her, his face sad.

'Finished!' Peter stood to bring his empty plate to the dish-washer.

'I'll take that,' said Mam. 'Why don't you and Simon go play some football out front? Your mum will be here soon, Simon.' She handed Simon back his now spotlessly clean shoes.

Peter wrinkled his nose. Hadn't he tolerated enough of Simon Sinclair for one day? He was tired and wanted to just flop in front of the telly. But he headed to the back door to get his coat and ball. At least the day was nearly over, so one final game of football wasn't too bad.

Simon sat down and slowly put his shoes on. He paused over the laces as if he was trying to think of something to say.

'Mrs Farrelly?' he said quietly.

'Yes, Simon?' Mam replied.

Simon paused. 'Nothing, just ... thank you for dinner.' He jumped up and rushed out the door, closing it behind him.

The kitchen was left in silence. Mam looked at the now empty chairs and couldn't help wondering if there was some-thing else Simon had wanted to say.

* * *

'Can I give you a flyer?'

Just like a bee, Kate was abuzz at the honesty boxes. Many

cars had been pulling in, eager to get fresh eggs … but also, it seemed, eager to get home.

'Eh no, thank you,' said one lady who barely looked her way.

'What flyer?' asked another gentleman. 'What bees?' He took the flyer, barely glanced at it, and threw it on the back seat of his already untidy car.

Another man rolled up his flyer and used it to swat away a fly that flew into his car.

Kate sighed sadly. 'They're not even listening to me, Maggie!'

'People are all in a hustle and a bustle,' said Maggie, trying to comfort her little helper. 'How about we put a flyer in each egg box? That way, they can read it when they're back at home.'

'Good idea!' said Kate, and she set to work adding flyers to the boxes.

A big Mercedes pulled up and Diane Sinclair rolled down her window. 'My goodness! What do we have here?'

'Would you like a flyer, Mrs Sinclair?' Kate asked hopefully, handing one in through the window. 'It's all about how we can help our bees. There are some great ideas for pollination, like growing flowers and not mowing our grass.'

'Why, of course I'll take one. In fact, give me a few of them so I can share them out.'

Diane loved this little girl's passion and enthusiasm – she hoped some of it had rubbed off on Simon during his day at Hazel Tree.

* * *

But back at the house, things were not going well with the football, and an argument was brewing.

'It wasn't a goal!' argued Peter. 'I blocked it with my leg.'

'It was over the line,' Simon snarled. 'You were too far back.'

'Give me the ball,' demanded Peter. 'It's my kick out.'

'No, it's my shot again,' Simon said, squaring up.

'I said give me my ball!' Peter stood his ground. He'd had enough of Simon and wasn't going to let him away with this. This was *his* house and *his* ball.

'Make me,' Simon smirked, before lunging at Peter.

Peter flinched, and Simon laughed. 'Coward.'

Peter could feel the anger rising up. He went for his ball again, but Simon moved to one side, tripping Peter with his foot.

Seeing his mother pull into the driveway, Simon put his hand out to help Peter up. 'Keep your mouth shut,' he whispered, 'or you'll be sorry.'

Peter shrugged off Simon's outstretched hand and got to his feet by himself.

'Did you fall, Peter?' Diane Sinclair said as she walked towards them.

Peter glanced at Simon. 'Yes, Mrs Sinclair, I fell.'

'I tackled him, Mum,' Simon said, smiling at his mother, 'and I won.'

Just then, Mam came out of the farmhouse. 'Will you come in for a cuppa, Diane?'

'Thank you, but we must be off. Derek is back this evening, and I want us all to have a nice family dinner before it gets too late.'

'I've already eaten,' said Simon grumpily.

'Well, I'm sure you could manage a slice of toast or something. Your dad would like that.'

'Fine,' said Simon as he skulked off to the car, slamming the door.

'I hope he was well behaved,' said Diane with a sigh, 'and not too much trouble for you, Peter.'

Peter gave a shy smile but said nothing.

'He was no trouble,' said Mam. 'In fact, he proved most useful when moving the sheep earlier. Maybe the healthy outdoor living could help.'

'Derek's away a lot,' said Diane in a low voice. 'They're shooting a new documentary in America, and it's taking up so much of his time. I worry about how all this is affecting Simon.'

'Our children are more resilient than we give them credit for,' said Mam, putting an arm around Peter's shoulder and giving him a squeeze. 'They can prove very capable.'

'Speaking of which,' said Diane, 'your Kate is quite the

influencer, isn't she? I got some of her flyers on the way in. What a marvellous idea.'

'Yes indeed,' said Mam with a smile. 'Once our Kate puts her mind to something, that's it!'

As they waved off the Sinclairs, Mam turned to Peter. 'So how was that for you?'

'Terrible,' said Peter, his shoulders slumping as he finally let out the day's tension. 'If I never see Simon Sinclair again, it will be too soon.'

* * *

Sitting in the car, Simon noticed his mobile phone lying beside him on the back seat. His mother had refused to let him bring it today, and it caused the biggest argument. But now he realised he hadn't given it a single thought all day, he had been so busy.

As they drove out of Hazel Tree, Simon took another glance at the front paddock, where the calves were lying in the sun. He watched the Coopers' chickens scratching in the dust.

Peter and Kate Farrelly have everything, he thought. *It's not fair.*

He switched on the phone, and the screen burst to life with new messages.

STEPHEN'S BIRTHDAY PARTY THIS SATURDAY, 2PM AT
BOUNCE-A-LOT

CAN'T WAIT   PIZZA TOO!!

WOO HOO   IT'LL BE EPIC

SHAME YOU CAN'T BE THERE SIMON

Great, another party he was missing because of this place. But Simon had a plan, a *brilliant* plan, and no one was going to stop him.

* * *

Back at the farm, Dad was finishing repairs to a shed wall. Some grouting had come away, making some of the bricks loose. He had mixed enough concrete to repair the loosened bricks, but there was still quite a bit left over. Not wanting to waste it, he remembered a spot where this extra cement could come in very useful.

He pushed the wheelbarrow over and found the rough patch of grass near the back door of the house. It could get very muddy in the winter months and Mam was always complaining about mucky footprints on the kitchen floor. Putting a hard surface over it would be just the job.

He noticed the new planter over to the side and smiled. *Kate's new bee garden*, he thought. *That planter will sit very nicely on this cement once it hardens.*

Tipping over the barrow, Dad poured the concrete, covering the grass in full. The grass was already quite short, so it was easy to smooth out. He placed old bricks here and there to make sure no hen claws or dog prints would ruin the lovely smooth surface.

He stood back and admired the job. *Perfect*, he thought. *Just perfect.*

Chapter 6

Going Once, Going Twice ...

The next morning dawned bright and dry, but tensions were high in the kitchen of Hazel Tree. Dad sat quietly, eating his toast and drinking his tea. Normally he'd be slurping away and scattering crumbs as he spoke, but not today.

He was always quiet on the day of the sheep sales.

Blue sat at his feet, her instincts telling her that her humans needed to be nurtured today.

'Morning!' Kate said cheerfully as she breezed downstairs and headed straight for the back door. After a poor start, her flyers had fared a little better yesterday, and she was feeling back on track and full of motivation.

Eamon had given her strict instructions to water her freshly planted seeds and, using a ruler, she was going to measure the grass in her new bee garden. She wanted to measure it each day to see how much it grew in a week.

'Arghhhhhhhhhhhhhhhhhhhhhhhhh!'

Kate's scream filled the kitchen. Dad spluttered out a mouthful of tea. Mam and Peter ran to the door, and Blue jumped up, barking and growling in fright.

'My grass, my grass!' came the wails from outside.

Kate was sobbing as she stared at the area which only yesterday had been green and full of potential but was now grey and bare. 'PETER WOZ ERE' was etched in the corner of the still-soft cement.

'Who did this? Who did this?' Kate screamed between her sobs.

Mam looked to Dad, whose face was as grey as the concrete in front of them.

'It was me,' he stuttered. 'I didn't know it was special to you, Kate.'

'It was part of my bee garden!' she cried. 'How *could* you?'

She barged past her parents and ran upstairs.

Dad looked to Mam, who shook her head. 'I didn't know!' he said defensively.

Mam went back into the house. She would have a tough job comforting Kate.

Dad noticed Peter placing Blue's paw in the cement beside his name. 'Hey!' he exclaimed.

'What?' said Peter. 'Blue wanted to sign it too.'

Woof! Blue agreed, her black speckled paw now even more

speckled with grey cement.

As she made her way upstairs to Kate's room, Mam's phone rang. It was Diane Sinclair. A few seconds later, Mam ran back outside, looking alarmed.

'Quick!' she called to Peter and Dad, throwing their jackets to them. 'The calves have escaped and they're running amok all over Greenway Manor!'

There wasn't a moment to lose. Dad called Eamon from the jeep, who ran out to meet them. He climbed into the front seat and quickly reached for his seat belt as Dad sped off. Blue sat in the back of the jeep with Peter. She was panting, excited and anxious about what was going on.

'How did they get out?' exclaimed Eamon. He sounded cross.

'I have no idea,' said Dad, 'but I bet they're trampling all over the lawns of Greenway, making a mess of the place.'

Eamon let out a short whistle. 'That might cost a few quid to fix.'

Dad sighed. 'More costs. And this morning of all mornings. We still have to get to the sales yard.'

The evidence of the calves' great escape was everywhere. Mud, poo and debris from the hedges were strewn all over the road that led to Greenway Manor.

As they drove up the avenue, Peter chewed his lip. He was worried, no, *terrified*, of the mess that lay ahead. They came around the final bend and saw the Sinclairs standing in formation, arms outstretched. Simon held a branch and was pointing to the grass paddocks at the front of the house.

Diane Sinclair was pushing the calves towards an open gate, while Derek blocked a possible escape route to the right.

As they got out of the car, they could hear Simon barking orders at his parents. 'Move in slow, Mum. Don't spook them. Watch your back, Dad! We don't want them getting behind you – we're in big trouble if that happens.'

Simon removed his red baseball cap to wipe the sweat from his forehead. He put it back on and quickly moved his position in line with the calves.

Dad and Eamon stood behind Derek, who smiled, relieved to see help arrive.

Blue immediately ran wide of the calves, keeping them together and moving them towards the gate. This was a big test, even for a dog as experienced as Blue.

Peter moved alongside Diane, who threw him one of her smiles, which were always so kind.

With Simon heading up the operation and under the watchful eye of Blue, the naughty calves ran through the open gate of the paddock, bucking and skipping as they did so.

'Hurrah!' yelled Derek, closing the gate.

'Whoo whoo!' cried out Diane.

'You are so embarrassing,' sighed Simon.

'We are so, so sorry,' exclaimed Dad. 'I don't know how they got out, and we'll pay for any damage.'

Derek raised his hand. 'No, not at all. It was just lucky our gate was open and they had the good sense to come up the driveway rather than stay on the road.'

'We can move them home from here,' said Eamon, 'but we'll really need to figure out how they got out.'

'Leave them be for now,' said Derek. 'They're doing us a favour grazing down this paddock.'

Peter looked around. Large tufts of muck and grass were scattered all over the lawn. The calves must have been charging all over the place. A fancy statue was lying on the ground, its arm broken off.

'One of the calves had an itchy backside,' Diane told Peter, as she followed his gaze. 'I caught her using that statue as a scratching post.' She beamed another big smile, reassuring him that she wasn't the least bit cross.

'Please let us pay you for that,' said Dad, when he saw the broken statue. But the Sinclairs wouldn't hear of it.

'Reminded me of my childhood, helping my dad and grandad,' said Diane. 'Although it was really Simon who saved the day.'

By now the calves had stopped their playing and were tucking into the green grass. One of them, calf 1360, made her way towards the fence where Simon was standing. She put her nose to his outstretched hand, gently sniffing him.

'I think you might have a talent there, son,' laughed Derek.

A glimmer of a smile came over Simon's face on hearing his father's praise.

'My work is going to seem very boring after all this excitement,' added Derek.

Simon's smile faded. 'But you're only back!' he snarled.

'Something has come up on set. The production team need me back sooner than I thought,' Derek explained.

'Whatever,' muttered Simon as he stormed off, leaving 1360 looking after him.

In a temper, he tore his red baseball cap from his head and threw it to the ground. Blue ran to where it lay and picked it up in her teeth. She trotted after Simon, nudging his hand to let him know she was there. Gingerly he took it from her. With a wagging tail, Blue returned to Peter, who patted her gently on the head.

'Will you come in for a cup of tea?' Diane asked.

'We'd love to, but another time perhaps,' said Dad. 'It's sales day, I'm afraid, and there's still so much to do. I'll ring you to arrange the collection of this lot, and thanks again for everything.'

He, Eamon and Peter made their way back to the jeep and headed for home. Peter watched Simon as he walked off towards the old yard at the back of the manor.

'I tell you, that young Simon has the makings of a livestock farmer,' laughed Eamon. 'We're lucky those calves didn't make their way down the Greenway Tunnel – they'd be halfway to Ballynoe Train Station by now.'

'The Greenway Tunnel?' asked Dad. 'That's long gone, surely.'

'No, Dad,' said Peter. 'It's still there, we saw it yesterday.'

'I remember my father telling me all about that tunnel when I was little,' said Dad. 'How it was used by farmers who worked the Greenway estate to move the livestock to the village on market day. They didn't have animal trailers and jeeps back then.'

'The first lady of the manor, Lady Greenway, was an awful snob, according to my grandmother,' chuckled Eamon. 'She was known to bring her carriage through that tunnel on her way to Sunday mass so she didn't have to look at any of the villagers.'

'Can it still be used?' Peter asked. 'Does it still go all the way to Ballynoe Station?'

'I doubt it,' said Eamon. 'The McAllisters took over Greenway nearly fifty years ago. They kept the house and gardens in good repair, but they weren't farmers. They sold off much of the farmland for building and roadworks. I would say it's been blocked off at this stage.'

'I wonder if the Sinclairs know about the tunnel?' asked Dad.

Eamon shrugged.

From the back seat, Peter said nothing. He didn't know about Mr and Mrs Sinclair, but he had a feeling Simon knew all about the Greenway Tunnel.

* * *

Back at Hazel Tree, Mam was working hard to comfort a devastated Kate, whose whole body shook from sobbing. 'Now, Kate, we have plenty more places that will make a wonderful bee garden, and you still have your lovely wildflowers to look forward to.'

Kate sat up on her bed, wiping her wet, snotty face with the tissue Mam handed to her.

'They will be lovely, when they grow.' Mam smiled at her again.

Kate smiled back. 'I suppose so,' she sighed.

'Why don't we go down together and give them their daily watering?' Mam took Kate's hand as they slid off the bed. 'They need plenty of water to get themselves going.'

Feeling better, Kate followed her mother back to the kitchen. As Mam started filling up the watering cans, Kate went out the back door.

'Arghhhhhhhhhhhhhhhhhhhhhhhhh!'

Once again, Kate's screams made Mam come running.

Hettie and the other hens were scurrying everywhere, as

Kate shooed them away from her planter which had soil and compost strewn all around it.

'They've eaten them!' Kate cried out. 'They've eaten all the wildflower seeds!'

Mam closed her eyes as an even more devastated Kate ran into her arms. Operation Plan Bee wasn't going to plan at all.

'I've an idea,' said Mam. 'Why don't we go to the sales yard with the others? You can get a burger and chips in the café.'

'And a fizzy orange?' the little voice asked.

'And a fizzy orange,' smiled Mam.

The jeep and trailer bounced over the gravelled surface as they parked to the rear of the holding pens at Ballynoe Livestock Mart.

Kate sat between Mam and Peter, with Eamon beside Dad in the front.

Dad found their allocated pen and he and Eamon unloaded the sheep. 'We'll sell them as one lot,' he said to Eamon. 'Might get a better price if they all go together.'

Eamon nodded his head in agreement. From what they had seen in the other pens, the Hazel Tree sheep had the best condition and fleece – they certainly looked like the pick of the bunch.

Once the sheep were in, they all headed to the main ring to

see how the other lots were doing.

'Lot 450 is on the market,' said a large man with a micro-phone, who stood high up over the ring. 'Forty-five, forty-five, fifty, fifty ...'

'€50 a sheep,' sighed Dad. 'That's desperate, doesn't even cover costs.'

'Bid up, bid up!' the voice crackled over the microphone.

'That's the auctioneer,' Eamon explained to Peter and Kate. 'When he says "on the market", it means they have reached a price the farmer is happy to sell them at.'

'What's a bid?' asked Kate, happy to have this distraction from her disastrous Operation Plan Bee.

'That's the price someone offers to buy them,' Eamon replied.

'Fifty-five, fifty-five,' came the auctioneer's voice. 'This is quality stock, you won't go wrong.'

Peter looked around. 'Who is bidding?' he asked Eamon. 'No one is saying anything.'

'Look at the body language,' Eamon whispered back.

A farmer standing across from them winked. 'Sixty,' called out the auctioneer, with a tiny nod in his direction.

Another farmer rubbed his eyebrow. 'Sixty-five,' boomed the auctioneer.

A third farmer tilted his chin. 'Seventy!' the auctioneer shouted triumphantly.

'That's a bit better,' said Mam hopefully.

'Seventy, seventy, seventy,' the voice called again.

Peter scanned the crowd. No more movement.

'Going once, going twice ...' The auctioneer banged his gavel, signalling the end of the auction, and the newly sold sheep were escorted out.

'What's our lot number, Dad?' Kate asked.

'455,' said Dad. 'We'd want a miracle between now and then.'

The next few lots didn't fare much better, with one going for as low as €45.

'Sure you couldn't keep a sheep for a week on €45,' said Eamon, sounding downbeat for the first time.

Soon, Lot 455 was up.

'This is us,' Mam whispered excitedly, squeezing Kate's hand. She had always loved going to the mart with her dad as a young girl. Her dad would give her some of the money from the animals he sold – he called it a 'luck penny' – and she would run to the sweet shop beside the mart to buy apple drops and pink bonbons.

'Beautiful Texel ewes from Hazel Tree Farm,' announced the auctioneer. 'This year's lambs, and a fine lot they are too.'

Peter glanced at Dad, who was looking down at his feet, and then at Eamon, who seemed to be mumbling a prayer under his breath. Kate shuffled in closer to her mother.

'Fifty, fifty, fifty,' the auctioneer started.

Peter looked around, hoping to see some action from the crowd. He didn't move a muscle, terrified that he would accidentally buy something by scratching his nose or rubbing his chin.

'Fifty-five, fifty-five, sixty.'

Peter's heart began to race. They were already at €60. He looked at his dad, whose face was blank.

The auctioneer glanced down to Dad, who shook his head.

'No, no,' said the auctioneer, 'these are not on the market yet. Surely someone can recognise quality when they see it.'

'What's a good price, Eamon?' Peter whispered.

'We'd want over €100 per sheep,' said Eamon. 'That would cover our costs and give us some profit.'

'But sixty is a long way from a hundred ... ' sighed Kate.

'Sixty-five, sixty-five, seventy, seventy.' The bids were going up.

The auctioneer looked again at Dad, who glanced at Eamon. Eamon nodded his head. Dad nodded back at the auctioneer.

'Lot 455 on the market at seventy,' he cried out. 'Seventy, seventy, seventy-five, eighty.'

'C'mon,' whispered Kate, closing her eyes. The bang of the auctioneer's gavel nearly made her jump out of her skin.

'€80 a sheep,' said Dad. 'Oh well, it could've been worse, I suppose.'

'Let's get a cup of tea,' said Eamon. 'We've earned that for sure.'

* * *

Over in the café area, as Peter and Kate supped on their fizzy orange and munched their burgers and chips, they listened to the conversations going on around them.

'It's a disaster,' mumbled one farmer.

'Sure what can we do?' answered another.

'Just have to keep going,' said a third.

'Everyone sounds so cross,' whispered Kate, as a big dollop of ketchup fell from her burger.

'I know,' said Peter. 'If we had the same money as the Sinclairs, Mam and Dad would be so much happier.'

* * *

'Simon?' Diane knocked at her son's bedroom door. 'Lunchtime.'

'I'm not hungry,' Simon snapped back.

Diane went to knock again.

'Leave him, love.' Derek was busy packing his suitcase. 'It'll only start another argument.'

'Your video call is in a few minutes,' Diane reminded him, 'so you'd better get set up. You know how unreliable the internet is here.'

Hearing his parents go downstairs, Simon turned his attention back to the screen on his laptop. He had found maps and

old pictures of Greenway Manor, and one in particular had really got his attention.

Grabbing his notebook, he took notes and printed off some of the pages. Suddenly the screen went blank. His father must be on a video call – it always caused the WiFi to go spotty.

'Not again,' he snarled and reached for his phone. A message from his best friend Trevor flashed up.

SIMON ARE YOU COMING BACK FOR BILLY'S PARTY?
YOU CAN'T MISS ANOTHER ONE.
IT'S GOING TO BE HUGE

Simon started typing, a smile spreading across his face as he did so:

I'LL BE THERE

* * *

The drive back to Hazel Tree felt faster. With no sheep in the trailer, the jeep bounced along the road, rattling over every bump and pothole.

'We'll get those calves ready in the coming months,' said Eamon. 'Then the lambing is back on in March, and by the looks of that ram Larry, we could have some great stock this time next year.'

'But can we keep going for that long?' asked Dad.

'David,' Mam whispered from the back seat, putting her finger to her lips when Dad looked back at her in the mirror. She didn't want the children hearing this conversation.

'Of course we can,' grinned Eamon, turning around in his seat. 'Hazel Tree always provides.'

'I can help too, Dad,' Peter spoke up. 'Me and Blue.'

'Me too, Dad,' shouted Kate. 'The honesty boxes are selling out every day.'

Dad smiled. 'You two already do enough, and anyway, your main job now is to get ready for school tomorrow.'

Peter groaned and Kate slumped back in her seat. They had forgotten that today was the last day of summer holidays. Tomorrow was back to school.

Chapter 7

Trinidad Corn Soup

'**S**ettle down, everyone!' Ms Keenan pleaded from the top of the classroom.

Emily Keenan didn't like the first day back to school either, especially with a class as giddy as this one.

'Quickly!' she called again. 'It shouldn't be taking this long. You should be in your places by now.'

Soon the din of voices and the scraping of table and chair legs along the floor died down. Twenty-four pairs of eyes were focused on the teacher, who folded her arms and adjusted the glasses on her nose.

'Now,' she continued in a calm tone, 'we have a new pupil starting with us today, and I want you all to give a real St Brendan's welcome to Simon Sinclair.'

There was a low gasp from the class and once again the sound of chair legs scaping on the floor as the children stretched up in their seats to get a closer look at the new kid.

Simon was standing next to Ms Keenan. He looked nervous.

'Simon has just moved to Ballynoe from Dublin,' said Ms Keenan. 'Are you staying in the village, Simon?'

Simon looked at the twenty-three sets of eyes that were now on him. (Only twenty-three, as Peter's eyes were fixed firmly on the floor.)

'No,' he answered hesitantly, 'a bit out of town, in Greenway Manor.'

'GREENWAY MANOR?' cried out Tommy Brennan.

Simon nodded.

'Wowwwww!' the class chorused.

'How lovely,' said Ms Keenan, trying to hide how impressed she actually was. 'There's some great history from the Greenway estate, we can learn more about it in class.'

'Are your parents loaded?' Seamus Tallan shouted up.

'Seamus!' Ms Keenan sounded annoyed. 'That is not an appropriate question.'

Simon smiled and shrugged his shoulders. 'They make TV programmes,' he answered, suddenly enjoying the attention.

Ms Keenan's eyes grew huge. The children gasped and leaned forward in their seats. Peter's heart sank. He didn't like where this was going.

'What kind of TV shows?' Ms Keenan asked. 'Anything we might have heard of?'

Simon listed off shows from the SoFun network. With each gasp and squeal of delight from his classmates, his smile grew bigger and his nerves disappeared.

Ms Keenan once again struggled to contain the children's giddiness, even though she herself was just as interested in finding out more. 'Now, now, that's enough! I think we should invite Mr and Mrs Sinclair to our next Careers Day, and they can tell us all about working in the world of television. Doesn't that sound exciting?'

Peter groaned. His parents also did Careers Day. Normally they brought in a sheep or lamb and talked about farming and being a vet. It always made him so proud. But this year he knew farm animals couldn't compete with the Sinclairs' exciting jobs, no matter how cute and woolly they were.

Ms Keenan directed Simon to join the class. He walked towards an empty seat at the back, and she turned to sit at her own desk.

Simon's new seat was next to Peter's.

'Sorry, Ms Keenan,' Simon said, staring straight at Peter, 'can I move? There's a bad smell in this area.'

Looking through notes on her desk, Ms Keenan was flustered and didn't see what was going on. 'Yes, yes,' she said, waving her hand in the air, 'just swap with someone else.'

Luckily, Peter's best friend Mark jumped straight up and swapped seats. *Could this day get any worse?* Peter thought glumly.

* * *

Meanwhile, down the hall, Kate's first day back at school wasn't going well either.

She cringed as she watched the gardener mowing the lawn and chopping up all the wildflowers. She yelped in horror as her teacher swatted at a bee while the rest of her class screamed hysterically, 'Wasp! Wasp!'

'It's a bee!' she cried out. 'It won't sting you if you leave it alone.'

But they weren't listening, so the only thing Kate could do was jump up and open a window for the tiny creature to fly out.

'Sit down, Kate Farrelly,' said Mr Dolan. 'I did not give you permission to leave your seat.'

Kate put her head down on her desk as Mr Dolan chased the bee out the window and calmed the other children. Her Operation Plan Bee was a disaster – it would take a miracle to get it back on track. Kate felt utterly miserable.

* * *

By lunchtime, Simon Sinclair was fast becoming the most popular boy at St Brendan's. The whole school knew about Simon, Greenway Manor, and the Sinclairs' TV shows, and it seemed like everyone wanted to be his best friend.

And Simon was loving it.

He was not used to getting so much attention from people. He stood against the back wall while a bunch of other boys gathered around him.

'Do you know Blake Wells from *Zoo Files*?' asked Seamus Tallan.

'Of course,' Simon said, rolling his eyes. 'He's always at our house.'

'What about Jemimah Dimmels from *Motor Max*?' asked Tommy Brennan.

'She's my mother's best friend,' smirked Simon.

'And Billy Daniels?' cried Stephen Carroll. 'He's so funny in *Prankz-n-Gigglez*.'

'Where do you think he gets his best prank ideas?' Simon answered, pointing to himself.

'You are so lucky, Simon,' added Brian Grey. 'I mean, you're practically famous.'

'I know,' said Simon, yawning at his adoring fans. 'Some of us have it, and some of us don't.' Simon shot a look in Peter's direction as he said this.

Boys who would have been Peter's friends hadn't spoken to him all day. Instead they were hanging around Simon and acting like he was the best thing since sliced bread. And Simon was using his new power to bring torment and misery to Peter.

Every time Peter walked by, Simon sniffed the air. 'Do you

smell that?' he would say loudly for everyone to hear. 'It's that awful smell again. It must be that Peter Farrelly.'

Then he'd point his finger in Peter's direction. 'Yes, yes! There he is! I knew it, it's Pongy Peter!'

This time, as Peter walked past, Simon led the giggling boys in a chant. 'Pongy Peter, Pongy Peter!'

Tears stung Peter's eyes, he felt so cross.

'Ignore them,' Mark told him, shooting a glare at the group. 'They're all so fake, only pretending to like him because of the whole TV thing. It's so stupid.'

Mark knew how awful things had been for Peter lately. His friend had told him all about his first meeting with Simon, the day of the school uniforms, and the play date from hell.

'I know,' said Peter miserably. 'They always seem to do it when no teacher is about. It makes me so mad.'

'Simon Sinclair will be old news in no time, you'll see,' said Mark with a smile. 'Come on, we still have some break time left.'

The two boys ran to the front of the schoolyard. Mark had his new football and was excited to show Peter the tricks he had learnt in his summer soccer camp. They dribbled the ball and kicked it back and forth.

'Catch this!' called Mark as he threw a kick so hard and fast it sent the ball skidding across the tarmac.

Peter ran after it, his eyes on the rolling ball until it came to a sudden stop … under Simon's foot. Simon rolled it back and forth, smiling menacingly at Peter as he did so.

'Can I have the ball?' Peter asked.

'What's the magic word?' said Simon, smirking. His group of new friends came up from behind.

'Please,' Peter answered. 'Can I have the ball, please?'

'Hey, that's my ball!' Mark called over.

'That's not nice,' said Simon. 'I'm new and you should be involving me in your games.'

'Yeah,' said Seamus.

'Let us play too,' said Tommy.

'We're nearly finished,' said Peter as calmly as he could. 'Bell will be ringing soon. We can play tomorrow.'

'Well, I'm taking the ball until then,' said Simon, reaching down and scooping it up.

'That's Mark's ball,' said Peter. 'Give it back to him.'

'Make me,' said Simon.

By now their raised voices had caught the attention of the other children.

From the other side of the yard, Kate watched the scene unfold. 'Oh no,' she whispered under her breath. 'Don't do it, Peter, don't do it.'

'I found it, David!'

Back at Hazel Tree, Eamon and Dad had been walking the calves' paddock to try and find the spot where they had snuck through and escaped.

Eamon spotted one part of the fence that was broken, revealing the tiniest of gaps, just big enough for a cheeky calf (or eleven) to get through.

With new posts and rails and barbed wire, the two men set to work to fix the fence. It was lucky the Sinclairs had allowed the animals to stay overnight at Greenway Manor, giving Dad and Eamon enough time to find the gap and make the necessary repairs.

They didn't want to risk any more 'great escapes', so instead of walking the calves back down the lane, they decided to hitch the cattle trailer to the jeep to bring them home.

There wasn't enough space for all eleven, so it would take two loads.

Over at Greenway Manor, Derek and Diane proved very helpful in loading the animals. In fact, it looked as if they enjoyed it.

'They are lovely calves,' remarked Derek as he lifted and closed the ramp with Dad. 'I envy your life.'

Dad was taken aback. Derek Sinclair envied his life, when he had so much and was so successful?

'It was wonderful to have some life around the place,' agreed

Diane. 'I think I'll miss them.'

'Well, they certainly enjoyed their time here,' laughed Eamon, looking at the paddock. The grass had been well munched and flattened down by the sunbathing cattle. The lawn was still looking worse for wear, although the fallen statue was back up (minus its arm).

'We think it looks better like that,' said Diane, laughing.

'How did yesterday's sales go, David?' Derek asked.

Dad shook his head. 'Not so good, I'm afraid. The market is suffering, and it will be a difficult time to weather for many farmers.'

'I'm sorry to hear that,' Derek said. 'Everyone in the world has to eat, you would think farming of all things would be the perfect business to be in.'

'Maybe we should try our hand at television,' said Eamon with a wink.

Derek laughed. 'Trust me, that is definitely *not* a good alternative!'

'When are you off again?' Eamon asked.

'Day after tomorrow. Simon isn't taking it well, but there are problems with our latest TV show. The script isn't finished, and we cannot find a suitable location for some of the shots. It's back to square one, I'm afraid.'

'It'll be ok.' Diane put her hand on her husband's shoulder. 'We'll figure it out.'

* * *

As they moved the calves back into their own paddock at Hazel Tree, Eamon and Dad watched them run and buck before finally settling down to graze.

Maggie had been re-stocking the honesty box and walked over to meet them. 'Come on, you two. It's lunchtime, and I have a big pot of Trinidad corn soup waiting.'

Over at Coopers', Mam joined them for a bowl of Maggie's delicious, creamy soup, and — as it often did recently — the happy chat soon turned to the more downbeat topic of the farm finances.

'Well, I can always do more hours in the surgery,' said Mam, buttering some homemade brown bread. 'Lots of farms are calving this time of year, and between calves and lambs, that will take us all the way to next summer. By then, we'll be starting to sell lambs again.'

'That would be a help,' said Dad, 'but you have so much on your plate already, Marian.'

'Well, between the honesty boxes and Kate's bee plan, we might have another flourishing business at Hazel Tree,' chuckled Maggie.

Mam and Dad looked at each other and winced.

'Oh no, what?' asked Maggie.

Mam told Maggie and Eamon about the latest catastrophes Kate's bee plan had faced: Dad pouring the concrete on her grass and the greedy hens tucking into the planter box of seeds.

'Poor little pet,' said Eamon, shaking his head. 'It's hard when you feel so passionate about something and things go wrong.'

'Hmmmm,' said Maggie, a grin spreading across her face, 'maybe there is something we can do to help my little Kate.'

'Oh no,' said Eamon with a fake-serious look. 'What are you up to, Maggie Cooper?'

Just then Mam's phone rang, and she frowned at the screen. 'It's St Brendan's School. Hello? Yes, this is Mrs Farrelly.'

Her face changed and her eyes grew large as she listened to the voice on the other end.

'We'll be right down,' she said, sounding cross. *Very* cross.

Peter and Simon were sitting outside Principal O'Malley's office. One of the teachers had rolled up some toilet paper and stuck it up Simon's bloody nose. Another had given Peter an icepack, which he pressed against his swollen cheek. Even though it stung a little, he kept it there, afraid of getting into even more trouble.

It was Mark and Seamus who had split up the fight, while Tommy ran to get a teacher. Now the two boys sat in silence, waiting for their parents to arrive. They glanced at each other

when they heard footsteps coming around the corner.

Mam and Dad looked furious, as did Derek Sinclair. Diane's eyes were red from crying.

'You are in big trouble, young man,' Derek said, pointing his finger at Simon.

'You both are,' said Dad, glaring at Peter.

The principal opened his door. 'Thank you all for coming,' he said, standing to one side and gesturing for them to enter.

The boys sat in the two seats facing Mr O'Malley's desk, and their parents stood behind them. 'We don't tolerate any fighting or bullying at St Brendan's,' the principal began, in his sternest voice. 'I am really shocked at your behaviour, Peter, and on the first day back too. As for you, Simon, you're new to St Brendan's. This is not a good first impression, is it?'

Simon shook his head.

'Answer Mr O'Malley,' Derek said angrily to his son.

'No, Mr O'Malley,' Simon whispered.

'What will their punishment be?' Mam asked, her voice also stern.

The principal removed his glasses and placed them on the table. He folded his hands and sat forward. 'Well, given the severity of their actions today' – he looked at each of the boys in turn – 'the only outcome can be suspension for the rest of the week. I will ask Ms Keenan to send on work for the boys to do at home. That way they won't fall behind.'

Peter's mouth opened wide in horror. *Suspension?* He had never been in this much trouble before. He looked over at Simon, who just sat there, staring straight ahead, the usual angry expression on his face.

Diane Sinclair started to sob.

Derek stood up, ushering Simon towards the door. 'Thank you, Mr O'Malley,' he said with authority. 'I can assure you this will *not* happen again.'

Peter watched as Simon picked up his bag and followed his parents out of the room.

'Peter,' said Dad, 'what do you have to say for yourself?'

Peter wanted to tell them everything, about how Simon wouldn't give back the ball, the name-calling and how he was turning the other boys against him – but he couldn't find the words.

'Sorry, Mr O'Malley,' he simply said. 'Sorry, Mam. Sorry, Dad.'

'I expect better from you, Peter,' said Mr O'Malley. 'I hope you have learnt your lesson here.'

As they made their way back to the car, Peter could see the Sinclairs up ahead. They were arguing. Derek was shouting at Simon and waving his arms in the air.

'Is this how you repay us for everything we do for you?' he cried. 'That's it, no more phone, computer games, no more TV, no more anything.'

'What do you care, you won't even be here!' Simon shouted back.

'Oh, stop it, the pair of you,' said Diane. 'We will discuss this when we get home.'

Peter turned to his parents, suddenly looking defeated. 'I am sorry. I don't know why I felt so angry.'

'I do,' said Mam. 'Simon pushed your buttons and you lashed out.'

'We have to work on that anger, Peter,' added Dad. He reached out and gave Peter a hug. 'We all get angry, but it never leads to good things.'

By the time they reached their car, Simon and his parents were already driving away. As Mam and Dad got inside, Peter spotted something lying on the ground near where the Sinclairs' car had been.

'Hang on,' he called to his parents as they were putting on their seatbelts.

He ran over and picked up a notebook that had Simon's name written in the corner. It must have fallen out of his schoolbag. Peter flicked through the pages.

'Peter, come on.' His father's voice made him look up. 'You're in enough trouble as it is, we have to get going.'

Peter hid the notebook in his bag. He'd be sure to give it to Simon next week.

Back home, Blue made a fuss of Peter when he came in –

she wasn't expecting to see her favourite human this early on a school day.

'Now, now Blue,' said Mam, 'Peter is in big trouble at the moment. Ok, young man, upstairs and change out of that school uniform. There is plenty of work you can be doing.'

Peter gave Blue one more cuddle. 'At least you're happy to see me,' he whispered into her soft, furry ear.

Peter wasn't the only one under strict instructions.

'No, Eamon, I need you to reverse back some more! I don't want anyone to see what I'm up to.'

Maggie had decided to take things into her own hands and get Kate's Operation Plan Bee back on track. By now the flyers were all gone, and when Maggie had asked about the one pinned up in Bedford's Business & School Supplies, she was disappointed with the answer.

'Sorry, Mrs Cooper,' Eoin had told her, 'we had to take it down to make room for our envelope promotion.'

Revving the engine of the tractor once more, Eamon reversed the trailer into position, blocking the view for anyone passing by. Maggie's Operation Plan Bee 2.0 was now in action, but it had to remain top secret until she was ready for the big reveal.

Pulling a piece of paper out of her pocket, Maggie handed

it to Eamon. 'TOP SECRET' was written on top.

'What's this for?' Eamon asked, scratching his head.

'It's your work for the next week, Eamon Cooper,' said Maggie with a grin, 'and remember, Kate must not find out what we're up to.'

'What *we're* up to?' Eamon laughed. 'This one is on you, Maggie Cooper. I'm just following orders.'

Chapter 8

Out of Ballynowhere

In the days since the fight, Peter couldn't believe that he missed going to school and was actually looking forward to going back. Luckily Kate was keeping him up to date on all the schoolyard gossip.

'Everyone's saying you broke Simon Sinclair's nose and knocked out his two front teeth,' she told him over breakfast one morning.

'No, of course I didn't,' said Peter. 'He just had a bit of a nosebleed, that's all.'

'No more fight talk,' said Mam, as she sent Kate off to catch the school bus and Peter off to do his homework.

You would think that staying home from school would be the best thing ever, but by the end of the week, Peter realised that it wasn't fun at all. Mam and Dad were keeping him busy feeding sheep and doing housework, and there was the mountain of schoolwork Ms Keenan had sent home.

Now, even on a Saturday, he still had lessons to do before heading back to school on Monday. He looked over at Kate

watching her animal programme. Peter wasn't allowed any TV while he was suspended, which had been really tough.

To take a break from all his schoolwork, Peter had been sneaking peeks at Simon's notebook. It was full of sketches and drawings, and some were actually pretty good. There were pictures of cars and airplanes and even a picture of the calf, 1360.

Peter hadn't told anyone that he found it, and he wondered if that was wrong. He shuddered to think how mad Simon would be if he knew Peter had it. He would have to sneak it into his schoolbag next week when he wasn't looking.

'What's that?' Kate was at the door.

Startled, Peter didn't have enough time to hide the notebook. He put his finger to his lips and beckoned for his sister to come in. 'Close the door!' he said in a loud whisper.

Excited that she was about to learn a big secret, Kate quietly closed the door and rushed to her brother's side.

Peter told her all about the day he found Simon's notebook and showed her the sketches and notes that were inside. He handed it to Kate so she could get a closer look.

As she flicked through the pages, one stood out from the rest. Kate opened the book wide to get a proper look. It was writing, and it looked like a list of some sort.

phone	torch
batteries	boots
gloves	raincoat
food	money

There was also a collection of numbers:

07.30 08.15 09.00 09.25

'I bet that's some kind of secret code,' said Peter.

'No,' said Kate. 'That's not a code, they're times.'

In school Kate had learnt all about the 24-hour clock. They had used a bus timetable to learn when the buses were arriving and leaving the station.

She turned the page over to see a map sketched on the back – it was a map of the entire Greenway estate.

She recognised the main house, the avenue and the old yard as well as the tunnel. She moved her finger from the point of the tunnel's entrance to where you exit. It ran for quite a distance, coming out not far from ...

'Ballynoe Train Station,' she read aloud.

Peter's eyes grew large. What was Simon Sinclair up to?

* * *

In the surgery at the back of the house, Mam had a lot of work to do too. If she was going to get some extra clients, she would have to start making phone calls.

Although she was worried about making ends meet, Mam was also looking forward to the challenge of doing more farm calls and caring for animals bigger than a gerbil or a cat.

This was a busy but wonderful time in the farming calendar. There was nothing better than helping to bring new life into the world, and seeing a freshly calved cow or a ewe licking her newborn lamb was always the best reward.

And there were many other reasons to be optimistic. The Coopers were a great support, reassuring them that all would be well. Eamon had seen many ups and downs on Hazel Tree Farm over the years!

The new calves were thriving and gaining weight on the grass and nut mix they were being fed. And Larry had turned into a fine ram, a purebred Texel. He was well built, with good shoulders and a long, wide back. His eyes were alert and he had a great character. If these traits made their way into his offspring, the Texels of Hazel Tree Farm would be of greater value, no doubt.

Over in the yard, Dad was wrapping up the morning duties. It had been an early start, and he would be happy to get home for a cup of tea and his second breakfast. His tummy rumbled at the thought.

After he checked the flock one final time, he turned his quad bike for home. In the distance, he saw the Sinclairs' Mercedes pull up at the front door of the farmhouse.

That's odd, he thought. He hoped there wasn't another problem with the boys.

Since the fight, there hadn't been much mention of Simon Sinclair. But from the little bit that Peter had told them (and the little bit more that Kate had told them), Dad and Mam realised that Simon had been making things very hard for Peter. Even though Dad didn't like Peter's approach, he was quite proud that his son had stood his ground against a bully.

Bringing the quad back to the yard, he could feel his mobile phone vibrating in his pocket. He turned off the engine and removed his helmet. He saw that it was Mam ringing.

'Hello?' he answered, hoping it was something to do with breakfast.

'David,' said Mam, with urgency in her voice, 'can you come home? It's Simon Sinclair, he's gone missing.'

The children had also heard the car in the driveway and ran to the window to see who it was.

'What are the Sinclairs doing here?' asked Peter. He quickly stashed the notebook under his pile of schoolbooks.

'I hope they are coming to apologise,' answered Kate. She was still very cross with Simon for being so mean to her brother. She didn't care any more about the Sinclairs' TV shows and was determined to not talk to Simon until he started being nicer.

Soon they could hear voices in the hallway, but they couldn't make out what was being said – the walls of Hazel Tree were old and very thick. Peter went to the door, pressing his ear against the solid wood. Kate followed.

As soon as they heard footsteps coming towards the room, they ran back to Peter's desk. Kate grabbed a maths book. 'Yes, two times twelve is …?' she asked Peter, pretending to be helping him with his schoolwork as Mam entered the room.

Seeing the worried look on her face, Kate lowered the maths book.

'You two better come with me,' said Mam, her voice serious. We may need your help.'

The children stood up and followed Mam back to the kitchen, where Dad, Derek and Diane were waiting.

By now Simon had been missing for a few hours. After the fight in school, Derek had postponed his trip back to America. He was due to fly out that morning and had knocked on Simon's bedroom door to say goodbye.

'But he wasn't there,' Diane explained, her face ashen. 'He's not even answering his phone.'

'The gardaí told us to wait,' said Derek. 'They said normally children come home themselves when they get cold and hungry.'

'We thought he might have come here,' Diane added. 'He

had such a lovely day with you all, we just thought …' Her voice faded away as she put her face into her hands.

'I'm so sorry,' said Dad. 'We haven't seen him since that day at the school.'

'We are sorry to barge in like this,' said Derek as Diane started to sob. 'We just couldn't sit at home any longer.'

Mam put her hand on Diane's shoulder. 'You did the right thing coming here,' she said. 'We'll find him.'

She tried to sound confident but felt a knot of worry in her stomach. 'Peter, Kate, are you sure you don't know where Simon might be?'

'No,' said Kate as Peter shook his head.

'What about those other boys in your class, Peter?' asked Derek. 'I think Simon mentioned a Tommy Brennan and a Seamus Tallan?'

Everyone was staring at Peter now. Again, he shook his head. 'Well, I don't think they were that friendly. He only met them on the first day of school.'

'We'll ring them anyway,' said Mam, reaching for her phone.

'We should never have moved,' said Derek, as he paced up and down the kitchen, clenching his mobile phone tightly. Suddenly it rang, and he anxiously looked at the number.

'Not again,' he snarled. 'Harry, I told you I am out of reach. My son is missing. Whatever it is, it has to wait.' He paused and listened. 'Well, you can tell that director he can find another job if that's his attitude.'

He hung up the phone and looked over to Diane. She smiled at him, tears rolling down her face.

There was a knock on the door, and they looked up to see Eamon and Maggie. Mam had called them over too, and the smell of Maggie's freshly cooked scones brought some comfort to the situation.

Through the open door, Peter could hear his Mam speaking on the phone outside. 'Well, if you see him or hear anything, will you call us immediately? Yeah, they're very worried … We all are. Yes, I believe the police have been called.'

Mam walked back into the kitchen, frowning. 'No, nothing from the Tallans or the Brennans.'

Diane once again put her head in her hands, her shoulders shaking as she sobbed. 'Where could he be? What if something has happened to him?'

'Were there no clues?' Eamon asked quietly. 'A note, or is there anything missing from his room?'

'No,' said Derek. 'Nothing, it's as if he just disappeared.'

Peter and Kate looked at each other. Peter cleared his throat. 'Is there a bag missing?'

The adults turned to look at him.

'Peter?' his mother asked. 'What do you know?'

Peter paused and Kate jumped in. 'We have to get something, don't we, Peter?'

The children ran from the kitchen, the adults not far behind.

In his room, Peter grabbed Simon's notebook, opening it on the page with the list and the numbers. He handed it to Derek Sinclair.

Diane and Derek looked confused. 'What is this?' Diane asked.

'It's Simon's notebook,' Peter replied. 'He dropped it outside school after our fight. We think this is a list of train times, and there's a map on the next page, a map of the old tunnel. The Greenway Tunnel.'

'The what?' the Sinclairs said together.

'I didn't understand it before, but now I do.' Kate's heart was racing as she spoke. 'I think Simon was planning to run away, and he's using the tunnel to escape.'

'That tunnel hasn't been used in over fifty years,' said Eamon, alarmed. 'There's no way of knowing if it's safe for walkers.'

'We need to get home immediately!' cried Diane.

'We'll call the guards on the way,' said Derek, halfway out the door. 'They can meet us at Greenway.'

'We'll come with you,' said Dad. The adults grabbed their coats and headed to their cars, with Kate and Peter following behind.

'Come on, Blue!' called Peter. 'You can come too.'

Drip, drip, drip.

The tunnel was so cold and damp, much more than Simon thought it would be. He pulled up the collar on his jacket, tightened his scarf, and lowered his red baseball cap over the tips of his ears. Why didn't he bring a woolly hat? It would be so much warmer than his baseball cap.

Brrrrrr! He shivered as his freezing hands touched against his ears. He had forgotten his gloves too. They were on his packing list, but since he lost his notebook he had to try and remember everything from memory. He dug his hands deeper into his pockets, trying to warm them up.

His runners were no good at blocking out the cold, and the dampness from the ground had found its way through the soles of his shoes, so now his toes were like little ice cubes. The grooved cement at the entrance to the tunnel had only run for a couple of metres before turning to a slippery, muddy mess.

SQUEEALCHH! SQUEEALCHH! SQUEEALCHH! SQUEEALCHH!

The sound became more rhythmic with each step he took. But after a while, he was quite glad to hear it, as it was company from the otherwise deafening silence that was all around him.

His rucksack was also a comfort, warm against his back. He had packed a change of clothes, some spare batteries for his torch, food (mostly snacks and cereal bars) and some water. He had money too, plenty of it.

Over the last few days, he had stolen money from his mother's purse. He was sure to do it gradually so as not to arouse suspicion. Not that his parents would notice much about him anyway – his mother had been far too consumed with moving house and his father consumed with work. Just thinking about his father made Simon feel mad.

He was always away, and even when he was at home, he was either locked in his office on the phone or shouting at his family to 'be quiet, I'm on a call'.

Was it really too much for him to spend time with his son? Could he not switch the phone off or get someone else to take over for a while? There were literally hundreds of people working for him – surely one of those lazy sods could do some work.

Simon had lied to Peter and Kate about going on fishing trips to the island in the middle of their lake. His father had barely been to the end of the lawn, let alone on a fishing trip with his son. His only son. But Simon wanted to make it sound like his dad was as good as all the other dads.

As good as Peter's dad. He scowled again when he thought of Peter. *Perfect Peter!*

Peter's dad was always there, and he had Eamon too. He pretty much had two dads, and Simon had nothing.

He snorted angrily, breaking the silence. His parents had made him do this. It was their fault he was here, in this cold, damp place.

Well, he was going to show them. This would make them sit up and take notice. He was going home, to his friends, to his old life, and he would never come back here again, NEVER.

He wondered how long it would take them to realise he was gone. His father was leaving that day, so he would be too busy arranging his diary to be bothered to check on him. As for his mother, it would be lunchtime at the earliest. She had been leaving his breakfast outside his bedroom door since he was suspended.

'A good rest will make everything better,' she used to say to the closed door. 'By the time you go back to school, you will feel like your old self again.'

But it wasn't rest he needed. He needed to get away from this place. He was glad he wouldn't be going back to that school. He liked the attention on the first day, but he knew those boys were only talking to him because of his dad. They didn't really care about him or want to get to know him.

Finding out this tunnel was real was the best thing that happened since he got here.

Before their move, his parents had tried to convince him of how exciting it would be living at Greenway Manor. They had shown him all these history pages on the internet. It was really boring until he found a whole section on the Greenway Tunnel.

There were old pictures of cattle and sheep emerging from

the tunnel on Ballynoe market day, with the farmers using oil lanterns to guide them. There were also photos of the Greenway family in their fancy carriage, using the tunnel to go about their daily business away from the prying eyes of the local people.

Simon started planning his great escape out of Ballynoe (or Ballynowhere, as he liked to call it) the moment he arrived. It was the perfect escape route. He knew he couldn't use the road, as he would be spotted by some nosy neighbour.

Finding the maps had been brilliant too. They told Simon how long the tunnel was, so he could work out how much time it would take to reach the train station. He downloaded the train timetable, and the early morning trains were his best chance.

It was all so easy.

However, it would have been easier if Simon hadn't lost his notebook.

He had written down all his plans and his packing list, and he stuck in a map of the tunnel. He was sure he had put it in his schoolbag, but when he checked, it was gone. He had searched everywhere. He hoped he hadn't left it in his parents' car, or they would know what he was up to and where he was.

SQQUUEEAALLLCCCHHHH!

'Urrrrgh!' he shouted as his shoe got stuck in the ground for the millionth time. He pressed his hand against the curved tunnel wall so he could free his foot from the swamp-like mud. It was the gloopiest, sloppiest, slimiest stuff he had ever come across.

'Urrgggggh!' he shouted again as he felt the furry moss, which was sodden and damp from the ever-dripping water.

This place is gross, he thought, drying his hand on the side of his jacket. He tapped the face of his digital watch. It was a fitness one that showed how many steps he had taken as well as the time. The numbers glowed gently on the screen. He had estimated that it would take about an hour to travel through the tunnel and on to the train station. Even with extra time for breaks, by his calculations, he should be nearly halfway there. He knew there was a train around 8.30am, if only he could remember for sure. Not to worry. He could get the next one, then he would finally be home, his *real* home.

He had done everything in his power to stop his parents from moving here, even trying to sabotage the sale of their old house. When people arrived for viewings, Simon hid in the wardrobes making 'whooooo' noises in the hope they would think it was haunted. He even flicked the lights on and off to make it extra spooky.

When that didn't work, he hid some of his mother's stinky blue cheese in drawers all around the house.

'What's that horrid smell?' the people would ask, covering their noses.

'It's positively wretched!' one man said as he bolted for the front door.

Simon's mother (or more like her exceptional sense of smell) finally sniffed out the problem.

'How did that get there?' exclaimed Derek as Diane threw a suspicious look at their son.

'We'll have to keep the windows open for days,' Diane said, clearly annoyed.

Simon had been made check and clean every drawer in the house. It was a full week before the rooms smelt normal again.

'I think it would be better if the house was empty for future viewings,' the snooty estate agent had said, annoyed that a whole week had been wasted thanks to Simon's pranks.

When the 'Paul Daly Removals' van arrived to pack up the house, Simon became more desperate, telling the men they were at the wrong house.

'You must be Simon,' Paul Daly chortled. 'The estate agent warned us about you.'

As they packed the boxes, Simon took them out of the van and snuck them behind the house. But Paul Daly was always one step ahead – or in this case, standing right behind him. 'Ahem! You can put that back, young man.'

There was nothing else Simon could do. He was thrilled when they got lost on the way to Greenway Manor – maybe his parents would see it as a sign and turn the car around and head for home.

But, oh no, they had to run into Peter Farrelly. Simon hated him immediately.

Suddenly his torchlight flickered and dimmed, bringing Simon back from his daydream.

'Come on,' he hissed, tapping the side of it with his hand. The light came back on, but only for a moment. It flickered twice more before finally going out altogether.

'Oh no,' Simon said through gritted teeth as he slapped the side of the torch again. But it was no good. It was dead, and Simon was plunged into darkness.

Luckily he had packed new batteries. He swung his rucksack from over his shoulders and opened the zip. The sound echoed around him. He reached inside and felt around.

Food, money, a toothbrush ... 'Batteries!' he exclaimed.

His hands were like ice as he fumbled clumsily with the packet. Finally he managed to wiggle out the two small batteries and unscrew the bottom of the torch. But as he tried to take out the old ones, his hand fumbled some more, causing the new batteries to slip from his grip and fall to the ground.

SPLATT!

'Aaaargh!' Simon said angrily. This was wasting time.

He bent down and felt along the ground for the batteries. But no matter how hard he tried, he couldn't find them.

But he had another idea. His phone had a torch. He could use that.

He reached for his back pocket, where he had slid his phone in earlier. But it wasn't there. He tried the other pocket, then his front pockets, and then the pockets of his jacket. There was no sign of it!

Simon now felt panic grow inside him. Maybe he had put it into the bag. He felt around all the objects in his rucksack a second, third and fourth time. But no phone.

He slumped down onto the cold, wet ground. He was now in total darkness, and without a phone, he was totally alone. How was he going to tell his friends he had arrived if he didn't have a phone? Who would pick him up? But there was another problem.

The blackness all around him was causing him to lose his sense of direction. Simon suddenly couldn't work out which way he had come and which way he was going. The coldness stung from the tip of his nose to the tips of his toes. He was miserable, and if the truth be known, he was scared.

He closed his eyes and tried to picture the tunnel map from memory. The route had been so straightforward when it was sketched out in front of him.

'I'm not giving up,' he said out loud, sounding braver than he felt.

He twisted the red baseball cap so the peak faced backwards, shielding his neck from the cold. He would keep moving forward and hope that the end of the tunnel wasn't too far away. He had been walking for ages – it couldn't be much further.

Standing up and slinging the bag over his shoulders, Simon pressed his hand against the cold, wet wall. He would use it as his guide.

The wall was slimy to the touch, but Simon was no longer disgusted by it. Now it was his friend and all he had to hold onto. Many of its bricks and stones were loose or had come away and fallen on the ground. They had been easy to spot and avoid in torchlight, but in darkness it was yet another hurdle Simon had to overcome. Sliding his feet along, he pushed the scattering of bricks out of his way. He was moving slowly now, taking careful steps.

SQUEEALCHH! SQUEEALCHH! SQUEEALCHH! SQUEEALCHH!

The noise was even louder in the pure darkness, as was Simon's shallow breathing. He strained his eyes for any sign of light ahead and tried to concentrate on his steps: one foot in front of the other.

Suddenly it was as if the ground disappeared from under him. The sudden jolt caused his hand to slip from the side of the wall and he fell awkwardly to the muddy ground below. Something sharp struck his forehead, just above his right eye.

'Ahhhh!' he cried out into the darkness.

Feeling a little shocked, Simon lay there for a few moments. Once he felt calmer, he removed his red cap and, with a quivering hand, moved his fingertips to where he felt the pain. Something warm and wet was trickling down his face. Was he bleeding?

Placing both hands on the ground, Simon tried to stand, but another pain shot through his body like a thousand knives. The awkward fall had caused him to twist his ankle, and it hurt so much.

He dragged himself backwards to the wall, where he could lean back. The pain in his ankle was the worst he had ever felt, and the blood from his head trickled into his eye. Wiping it away, he squinted. Even the smallest shred of light would help him work out where he was. But he was in total darkness, and totally out of ideas. Simon was well and truly stuck.

'Help! Help!' he cried out, hoping that somehow, someone would hear him.

He clutched his rucksack against his chest, trying to keep warm and keep his mind off the pain from his ankle and forehead. He took out one of the cereal bars he had brought. He didn't know how long he would be here, so he had better keep his strength up.

As the time passed – he couldn't tell how long – Simon reached into his bag for another snack, only to realise he had eaten the last of his bars. He didn't have another morsel. *Why didn't I bring more?* he thought, his eyes filling with tears.

As he continued to lie there, his ankle throbbed and his forehead felt tight as the blood began to dry. At least that was something to be thankful for.

Surrounded by darkness and empty wrappers, he tried to keep upbeat. He called out again. Maybe by now his parents had noticed he was gone and were looking for him.

Drip, Drip, Throb Throb

With the loss of his sight, Simon's other senses were heightened. The smell of the mud and damp, along with the sounds and the pain pulsating through his body, were nearly too much to bear. He opened his eyes as wide as he could, pleading with them to make out something in the pitch black.

'Come on, come on ...' He strained them further. But it was no use.

'It's pointless,' he sobbed.

Suddenly his ears picked up something. It wasn't the dripping but something familiar. Had he just heard his name?

He wanted to believe it ... but was his mind playing tricks on him? Was it just his imagination?

But what if it wasn't?

'Help! Help!' he called. 'I'm here! Can anyone hear me?'

Straining his ears, he tried to move in the direction of the sound. He cried out again as the pain ran through his body.

As his echoes died down, Simon was left in the silent

darkness once again. He put his face in his hands and started to cry. It was no good. No one could hear him, and no one knew where he was.

'No, I can't give up!'

Somehow, Simon found a shred of courage. Wiping his tears, he strained his ears and eyes once more.

Drip Drip, pitter, drip, patter, drip, pitter, patter, drip … pitter pattter, pitter patter

Was it just his heart racing? But no, Simon felt a presence. He was no longer alone. He gasped. Whatever it was, it was coming towards him. He reached a quivering hand out in front of him.

'Who's there?' he cried, his hand punching the darkness.

Suddenly something warm and hairy brushed against his fingertips. Startled, Simon jerked his hand back.

'Get away!' he called into the darkness. But the large, hairy thing brushed past him once again, closer this time.

Simon felt something wet licking his face and then pushing or nudging against him. He shot back in alarm, ignoring the pain as he did so. The face-licking stopped, and Simon reached out again, with both hands this time, to feel the warm, silky fur of an animal. Was it a dog?

The licking moved from his face to his hands, before suddenly stopping altogether. Simon got the terrible feeling that he was alone once more.

'Come back!' Simon cried. 'Please come back!'

Chapter 9

Garda Blue

It was nearly ten o'clock when the five gardaí and their trained sniffer dogs arrived at Greenway Manor. The sight of the police and dogs alarmed Diane and Derek even further.

'Those dogs will find him in no time,' Dad said, trying to sound reassuring.

Blue yelped with excitement on seeing the dogs, sensing that something big was afoot.

'Leave Blue in the jeep, Peter,' warned Mam. 'We don't want her getting in the way of the police dogs.'

'Sorry, Blue,' said Peter, closing the door of the jeep. Blue popped her head out of the open window and barked after him. He put his finger to his lips. 'Shhhhh! You have to stay there, you'll only get in the way.'

Knowing it was no use, Blue lay down on the back seat, placing her disgruntled head on her front paws.

Sgt Louise Curtin was in charge of the rescue operation. She looked at the notebook that Peter had shown the adults. 'These are train times,' she said when she saw the numbers.

She beckoned to her colleague. 'Call the train station and have them check all CCTV immediately. We need to see if Simon made any of these trains.'

'Yes, Sarge,' said the garda before rushing back to the car to make the calls.

The Sinclairs had been asked for an item of Simon's clothing so the dogs could get a scent. Diane brought a hoodie and handed it over. The two dogs sniffed it before excitedly pulling their handlers in the direction of the old yard.

'They've picked up the scent,' said Eamon.

Derek and Diane took off after the dog handlers, and the Farrellys and Coopers tried to keep up.

'Best not to get too close,' said Eamon, a little out of puff. 'We'll put the dogs off the scent.'

In the back seat of the jeep, Blue sat upright. Her senses were on full alert too. She pushed her head through the open window and barked after the others, who were now disappearing into the distance. Upset and anxious, she whimpered and ran up and down the back seat.

She couldn't stay here. Something was up and she needed to be in the middle of the action.

A crunch of gravel nearby meant someone was coming. Blue's ears pricked as she heard the car door click, and she cocked her head to one side, working out what the sounds might mean. As the door swung open, there stood Kate. She felt so bad for poor Blue, she had snuck back to get her.

'It's ok, Blue. I'm here, you can come with me. But we must be on our best behaviour.' Kate placed her hand on Blue's collar and helped her down, only taking her hand off the collar to close the jeep door.

Seeing her chance, Blue took off at great speed to catch up with the others.

'Blue!' called Kate. 'You're going to get us in trouble!'

But by now, the sheepdog was just a dot in the distance.

* * *

The sniffer dogs led the group to the opening of the tunnel.

'I never knew this was here,' said Derek.

'Well, someone did,' said Sgt Curtin, pointing down at the footprints. 'Someone has cleared away a lot of the weeds too.'

One of the gardaí crouched down and recovered something from the muddy entrance of the tunnel. It was a slim black mobile phone.

'That's Simon's!' cried Diane in alarm. 'He would never be without that phone.'

Suddenly Sgt Curtin's walkie talkie crackled on her shoulder.

'Sgt Curtin, do you read me?' came the voice on the other end.

'Yes, go ahead,' she replied.

'All clear at the train station,' the voice continued. 'There has been no sighting of Simon Sinclair to date. All the train drivers have been notified to be on the alert.'

'Ok. Stay on the radio and alert us to any updates.' Sgt Curtin sounded worried now.

Diane looked to Derek in alarm. If Simon never made it to the train station, then it was highly likely he was somewhere in the tunnel.

Taking a torch from her belt, Sgt Curtin pointed it at the tunnel's entrance. The light illuminated the stone ramp that led downwards to the damp, muddy passage below.

The dogs whimpered. They were anxious to get into the tunnel. They strained at their leads, but the handlers didn't move.

'What'll we do, Sarge?' one of them asked, struggling to hold his dog.

Sgt Curtin stood back. 'We have no idea what kind of condition that tunnel is in. It mightn't be safe.'

'But you have to go in,' said Diane, almost hysterical now. 'My son could be in there.'

'Well, I'm going in,' said Derek, trying to push past the police.

Sgt Curtin put her hand up and stopped him. 'Mr Sinclair, I understand your worry, but trust us, we need to know more about what we are facing by going into that tunnel.'

Peter suddenly felt something nudge his hand. 'Blue,' he

whispered, 'what are you doing here?'

As a sheepish Kate arrived beside her parents, Mam rolled her eyes in disapproval.

'She wanted to come,' Kate insisted.

'Keep a tight hand on her, Peter,' said Dad. 'She mustn't get in the way.'

Knowing her place, Blue sat obediently as Peter kept hold of her collar. Eamon came forward, unwrapping a length of old baling twine he found in his pocket.

'A good farmer is never short of baling twine for an emergency,' he said as he created a lead for the mischievous sheepdog.

Sgt Curtin beckoned to another garda who was holding a loudspeaker. 'We'll see if Simon can hear us first and then we'll see about heading in.' She turned her face to the walkie talkie and spoke quietly to the garda on the other end. 'Get the paramedics on standby.'

The garda with the loudspeaker flicked a switch before handing it to Sgt Curtin. The feedback made them all jump, including Blue, who gave out a small bark in disapproval. Peter gently tugged on her twine lead, asking her to settle.

Sgt Curtin signalled for everyone to be quiet. Carefully she stepped onto the ramp and took a few steps into the darkness. She placed the loudspeaker to her lips.

'Simon? Simon, can you hear us?' she called into the black hole ahead of her.

Nothing.

Once again, Sgt Curtin spoke into the loudspeaker, this time louder. 'Simon! Simon, can you hear us? Shout if you can hear us.'

Still nothing.

Diane began to sob, and Maggie pressed her hands together in fear.

Blue was sniffing the ground around her and whimpering.

'Shhhhh, Blue,' Kate whispered. 'I'll have to take you back to the jeep if you don't behave.'

Blue nudged Peter and pulled in the direction of the tunnel.

'Blue,' said Peter, 'you have to behave.'

Peter looked down at his dog and suddenly had that familiar feeling that she was trying to tell him something. He glanced over at the adults, who were talking with Sgt Curtin and the rest of the gardaí at the entrance of the tunnel.

Peter had an idea. Carefully and quietly, he untied the twine from Blue's collar. In a nanosecond, she darted past his parents, the Coopers, the Sinclairs and the gardaí. Sgt Curtin was pushed backwards against the wall of the tunnel as Blue whisked past her. The startled police dogs tried to follow.

'Peter!' cried Mam. 'What have you done?'

'She'll be lost,' shouted Dad.

'Wait! I think she might be on to something,' said Eamon, his eyes wide.

With that, everyone – humans and dogs – peered into the tunnel after Blue, who by now was nowhere to be seen.

Sgt Curtin switched her torch back on. She moved into the tunnel entrance. Every step she took, it felt colder and damper. The ramp was also getting more slippery, with the moss and algae from the damp conditions. She pointed her torch, trying to see as far ahead as she could. Blue was well and truly gone at this stage. It was as if she had vanished into thin air.

'That dog should never have been let off the lead,' Sgt Curtin said to Peter, the anger in her voice rising. 'We don't need a lost dog added to our list.'

'I'm sorry,' said Peter desperately, 'but I think she senses something. I just had a feeling.'

Peter looked to his parents and the Sinclairs. 'I'm sorry,' he pleaded. 'I thought it would help.'

Kate comforted her brother. 'I'd have done the exact same thing,' she whispered.

Eamon spoke up. 'The dark won't bother Blue. That dog has done some of her best work at night.'

'That is correct,' added Maggie. 'Many a lost lamb she has found in the dark. Let's give her a chance.'

Sgt Curtin shone her torch into the tunnel once more, straining her eyes to get the first glimpse of something, anything. She sighed. It seemed she had no other choice but to send in the dogs and handlers. It was a risky move, as no one knew what lay beyond that darkness.

Sgt Curtin began issuing orders and arranging who was to go in first. She was only midway through her briefing, pointing her torch into the tunnel, when suddenly two spots of white light came into view. It was Blue, her eyes reflecting back the torchlight. As she reached Sgt Curtin, Blue dropped what she was carrying in her mouth. Sgt Curtin reached down and picked up a red baseball cap.

'That's Simon's!' roared Diane.

This was all Sgt Curtin needed to hear. 'He's down there!' she called out. 'Get the dogs ready.'

Blue didn't need to be told twice. She swung around on her paws and ran back into the tunnel.

Sgt Curtin, the gardaí and the dogs followed Blue along the passage. Sgt Curtin and another garda held their torches in their hands, while the handlers had lights strapped to their foreheads. The ancient stone walls of the tunnel were bathed in light now. The damp moss shimmered, and in many places, they could see fallen stones and bricks littering their way.

Over the years, the rising damp and lack of care had caused the structure of the tunnel to weaken and fall into disrepair. Sgt Curtin knew only too well that this was not somewhere

they should be walking, let alone a little boy. She hoped they were not too late.

The light cut through the darkness, bouncing off the walls as they hurried to keep up with Blue. Sgt Curtin spotted something shining up from the mud, something out of place, and she stooped down to pick it up. A battery – two, in fact – and they looked new and unused. Had Simon tried to change his torch batteries? Was he down here in complete darkness?

'There, up ahead!' cried one of the handlers.

It was Simon, lying against the wall, his backpack beside him. As the torchlights shone in his direction, he lifted his hand to shield his eyes. He was pale, and the light picked up the large gash on his forehead. He smiled when he saw Blue.

'Am I dreaming again?' he said, his voice weak.

Blue licked his cheeks as he sobbed, tears streaming down his muddied, bloodied face.

It hadn't been a dream. It was Blue, and she had come back for him.

'I'm Louise,' Sgt Curtin said, kneeling down beside him. 'Are you badly hurt?'

'I fell,' said Simon. 'My torch stopped working and I didn't know how to get out. I think I fell over something.'

Sgt Curtin moved her torch along the ground. It was very uneven, with stones and bricks scattered everywhere. Simon must have lost his footing and banged his head on the stones.

He could have a concussion, she thought to herself. She shone her light along his legs to see his swollen ankle, which looked to be broken.

'We're going to get you out of here,' she said, smiling broadly.

Throwing Simon's rucksack on her back, and with her torch sticking out of her pocket, she beckoned to her colleague. Facing each other with Simon in the middle, they crouched down. They took each other's wrists and shoulders, creating an area for Simon to sit in. Simon gently edged into position, placing his arms around the shoulders of the two gardaí.

Once in place, they rose slowly to their feet, cradling the exhausted but delighted Simon in their arms. His head rested against Sgt Curtin.

Instinctively Blue took up the lead, followed by the two sniffer dogs and their handlers, with Simon and his carriers following closely behind.

It wasn't until they were closer to the entrance that they could finally be heard shouting that they had found Simon. Blue emerged first, followed by the rest of the crew. Peter and Kate ran straight to her, giving her huge hugs and snuggles.

'You did great!' Kate gushed.

'You're such a great girl, such a great girl,' cried Peter.

Peter looked over at Simon. He was weak and pale. Peter

suddenly didn't see a boy who was mean and spiteful. He was surprised at how sorry he felt for him.

Diane and Derek ran to their son. Through her tears, Diane stroked his hair. 'Are you alright, darling? Are you alright?'

Simon gently nodded his head.

'I was so worried,' Derek said, choking back his tears.

'Dad,' Simon said in a weak voice, 'you're here.'

'Of course I am.' Derek's voice quivered as tears rolled down his face. 'I will always be here.'

Eamon handed Maggie his handkerchief. She too had tears in her eyes as she watched the Sinclairs with their son.

The gardaí alerted the ambulance, and soon the paramedics were on the scene with a stretcher and oxygen mask. Simon was placed onto the stretcher as the medics tended to him.

As Simon was being loaded into the ambulance, Derek and Diane thanked Sgt Curtin and the gardaí and gave Blue a well-earned pat on the head. Diane got into the ambulance with Simon, and Derek followed behind in the car.

As the ambulance disappeared from view, Maggie put her arms around Peter and Kate. 'Well, I don't know about you,' she said, 'but I could do with a cup of tea.'

'Or a second breakfast,' said Dad, his rumbling stomach reminding him he was still hungry.

In the back seat of the jeep, Blue snuggled in between

Peter and Kate. Her tummy was grumbling too. It wasn't just Dad who had missed his second breakfast.

Chapter 10

A Hero's Welcome

'Oh Diane, that is great news! We are all so glad.' Mam's voice carried along the hall and up the stairs to Peter and Kate's bedrooms. They were just getting up after a lazy start to their Saturday morning.

As they came down for breakfast, Hettie could be heard at the back door trying to get in.

'I have just been on the phone to Diane Sinclair,' Mam told them as she took milk out of the fridge. 'Simon is doing really well since he left hospital and will be right as rain in no time.'

'Will he have to wear a cast on his leg?' asked Kate, nibbling on her toast.

'Oh yes,' said Mam. 'His ankle was badly broken. He'll be in a cast for a few weeks, and he had to get stitches for the cut on his forehead.'

She paused as she placed the milk on the table. 'He's extremely lucky. Who knows what would have happened if we hadn't found him when we did.'

Peter looked over at Blue and smiled. It was all thanks to

Blue that they had found Simon. Without her, things could have been much worse.

'But that's not all,' Mam continued. 'Diane was actually ringing to invite us to a special party at Greenway Manor. They think it's about time they got to meet everyone in Ballynoe, and they want Blue to be their guest of honour.'

Blue's tail wagged as she heard her name.

Kate wriggled with excitement. 'Will there be a bouncy castle there? Or maybe a magician?'

Mam smiled. 'I don't know. We'll just have to wait and see.'

It had been a week since the tunnel rescue, and Peter hadn't seen nor spoken to Simon in all that time. He was on bedrest due to his injuries so he hadn't been back at school, which, for Peter, had been absolutely wonderful. A whole week of not having to worry about bumping into Simon Sinclair.

Anyway, Peter was the one everybody wanted to talk to now. The whole school had heard what happened and how clever Blue had been in leading the gardaí and their sniffer dogs to Simon.

But hearing that Simon was out of hospital, Peter began to worry again. Would he still be nasty when he got back to school? Would Peter have to keep his distance once more?

'I thought we could go into town and get Simon a little present,' Mam said, interrupting Peter's thoughts. 'And maybe we can get some more flyers printed, Kate?'

Kate put her toast down and gloomily rested her face against her hand. 'What's the point?' she said sadly. 'No one cares.'

'Well, maybe they just need more time,' said Mam.

'Nope,' said Kate. 'Operation Plan Bee is no more.'

With breakfast finished, the children were helping to tidy the dishes when Mam's phone rang. It was Maggie.

'Oh no!' Mam cried. 'Maggie, we'll be right there.'

The children looked at each other.

What now?

'Quickly!' exclaimed Mam. 'There's a problem at Coopers'.'

Peter and Kate jumped up and all three, along with Blue, took off towards Cooper's Farm. They took the shortcut through the hedge, which brought them straight past the chicken house and into the main yard.

Dad and Eamon were already there, and Maggie was in a terrible fuss. 'Oh, thank goodness you're here,' she exclaimed. 'We're missing eight hens. We've been searching everywhere.'

'I hope it's not another fox,' said Kate, alarmed.

'Don't worry, Maggie,' said Mam. 'We'll help you find them. They can't have gotten far.'

If the children, especially Kate, had been paying attention, they would have seen the wink the two ladies exchanged.

Dad, Eamon and Peter went to the left, while Maggie, Kate and Mam went right.

'We'll meet back at the main gate,' said Eamon, doing his

best to hide a smile.

'Where were they last seen?' Kate asked Maggie.

'Over by the workshop,' Maggie answered. 'We could start there, I suppose.'

Kate took the lead. 'We'll search for clues. That'll lead us straight to them, just you see.'

The trio headed to the workshop and soon saw their first clue – some chicken grain was scattered by the door.

Kate pondered for a while, tapping her cheek with her finger. 'This must be where they had their breakfast!' she said triumphantly. She looked around and soon saw another clue, a tail feather sticking up out of the ground. 'This way!'

Mam and Maggie followed her, doing their best to keep up and hold their giggles in.

There were more clues along the way: some freshly dug-up soil ('They must have been hunting for worms!') and a dusty patch of gravel ('They stopped here for a sand bath!').

Finally, super sleuth Kate's trail of clues led her to the old apple orchard at the side of Cooper's Cottage. Kate had always loved how the pink and white blossoms looked in the springtime. The orchard was enclosed by a small stone wall and only accessible through a pretty iron gate. Today, however, the pretty gate was blocked by Eamon's tractor and trailer.

In fact, for some strange reason, Eamon had left his trac-tor parked here for quite some time. It had annoyed Kate a little, as those coming to the honesty boxes by the main gate couldn't see the loveliness of the orchard. But now, she was even more annoyed as it was preventing her from solving the mystery of the missing hens.

She spun on her heels to face Mam and Maggie, who were standing back, wondering what to do next. 'It's quite simple,' started Kate. 'If my hunch is correct, and I'm sure it is, your hens are somewhere in the orchard. The only problem is we need to move this big heap to get in.'

'Your wish is my command.' Eamon's voice made Kate turn back around. He hopped up onto the seat of the tractor with a huge smile on his face.

VROOOM VROOOM!

He revved the engine, and slowly the tractor moved forward, pulling the trailer with it.

Before Kate's very eyes, the orchard reappeared – but it wasn't the orchard as she remembered it.

With huge grins on their faces, Dad and Peter were standing next to a sign that read:

'The Operation Plan Bee Garden'

The grass in the orchard hadn't been mowed and was the longest Kate had ever seen it, perfect for sheltering bees. The planter from the back door was set up beside the gate. Fresh compost had been added and there were already little shoots of flowers to be seen.

Kate's eyes were wide with wonder as she scanned this thrilling view. Soon her gaze rested on a large object that sat opposite the planter. It was covered with a sheet.

'What's under the sheet?' she asked, her voice quivering with excitement.

Knowing that this was his part in the big reveal, Peter ran to the gate. He picked up a corner of the sheet and, clearing his throat, made a small trumpet sound. 'Perump pah pah!'

He pulled the corner of the sheet so it slid off to uncover a large, beautifully crafted bee hotel.

It was shaped like a doll's house and broken into compartments of bamboo and hollowed-out tubes. Wooden blocks with drill holes and mesh areas would all provide solitary bees a safe space to build their nests and hatch their eggs.

'Who ... what ... how?' For once, Kate was stuck for words.

Eamon and Mam walked together towards the gate. Standing at each pillar, they unrolled a long red ribbon. Maggie stood beside the astounded Kate and handed her a pair of scissors.

'You really inspired us with all your work, Kate,' Maggie explained. 'Will you please do us the honour of officially opening The Operation Plan Bee Garden?'

Taking the scissors, Kate snipped the ribbon held by Eamon and Mam.

A big cheer rang up and everyone clapped.

'Now when people come to the honesty boxes, they will not only be able to read about Operation Plan Bee, but they'll also be able to see it in action!' Maggie explained, joyously.

With tears in her eyes, Kate ran and hugged Maggie and then Eamon. Mam, Dad and Peter joined in for one big group hug, while Blue barked and jumped with glee and Hettie made a beeline for the planter.

'I don't think so, Ms Hettie,' Maggie said, scooping up the cheeky hen and placing her on the ground near a nice pile of clay. 'No more flower seeds for you!

'Thank you, thank you,' Kate whispered between her happy sobs.

Eamon reached into his pocket and took out a packet of wildflower seeds. 'We still have some seeds left over, and it's not too late to sow them.'

Kate beamed. She felt like her heart was going to burst with joy. Her dream of a bee garden had come true.

The following week was a happy one at Hazel Tree. Happier than it had been for some time.

Kate was busy making plans for her new bee garden. She and Eamon had sown the wildflower seeds, and Maggie was keeping a careful eye on Hettie and the rest of the hens. Kate couldn't wait to see the garden in full bloom.

Larry had been put out with the ewes, and the calves were thriving. They were also staying where they should, safe and sound in their paddock, largely due to the electric fence Dad and Eamon had put up.

Mam was busy with her new patients, which included a bull with a sore tooth and a horse with tummy ache.

'Colic,' she explained to the horse's worried family. 'We'll soon have him right as rain, with some medicine and plenty of walking to get everything moving again.'

By the day of the Greenway Manor party, everyone was in high spirits. Driving up the manor's majestic avenue was never a dull experience, and Blue, with a pretty bow on her collar, could feel the excitement. From the back seat of the jeep, she took turns first licking Peter's face and then Kate's.

'Oh, Blue!' giggled Kate. 'Stop putting your slobber all over me and my nice clothes!'

While everyone was excited, Peter couldn't help but feel a little bit nervous too. This would be his first time to see Simon since the day of the rescue. He placed his hand on his tummy to ease the familiar flutters that suddenly appeared.

There were already plenty of cars parked along the avenue, and the Sinclairs had opened the paddocks for extra parking. It seemed like the whole of Ballynoe was here, eager no doubt for a chance to see Greenway Manor for themselves.

Dad found a place to park, and Maggie and Eamon pulled

in behind. Blue was put on her lead, and Mam ran to help Maggie with the huge haul of food and treats she had brought.

'I don't know why you did all this,' Eamon grumbled as Maggie handed him a large box crammed full of foil-wrapped packages.

'It's bad manners to come to a home empty-handed,' scolded Maggie. 'I am sure Diane will appreciate some of my Caribbean delights.'

Dad pointed over at the huge van with 'Gourmet Catering' emblazoned on the side. 'It looks like the Sinclairs have all the food they could possibly need,' he whispered to Mam.

'Shhhhh,' said Mam, with a smile. 'You know how much Maggie loves to cook. No doubt she'll give those caterers a run for their money.'

They made their way to the main entrance and up the steps to the fine hall of the manor, where there were balloons and bunting galore.

'Welcome, welcome!' Diane met them and embraced her friends with open arms. 'We are so glad you are all here.' She placed her hand on Blue's head and tenderly patted and rubbed the young dog. 'And of course you, Blue, our special guest of honour.'

Diane led them to a large room with glass doors that opened onto the magnificent lawns and gardens.

'Wow,' said Kate.

Before them was a party like no one had ever seen. There was an ice-cream van, candy floss and popcorn makers, clowns making balloon animals, and magicians doing card tricks and pulling coins from people's ears.

There was not one but *three* bouncy castles and a helter-skelter with children (and some adults) zooming down in potato sacks.

'Go on, you two!' Mam pushed the children towards the door. 'Go and enjoy yourselves.'

She reached into her jacket pocket and took out some small plastic bags, which she handed to Peter and Kate. 'And these are for Blue,' she whispered. 'Let's be sure the guest of honour doesn't leave presents of her own on that lovely lawn.'

Wincing at the thought, the children took the bags and, along with Blue, they ran outside to join the fun.

Peter's whole class was there, and in the distance, he could see many of them gathered in a huddle. They were laughing and tucking into ice cream and popcorn. In the middle of it all sat Simon Sinclair, a bandage around his head and the lower half of his leg in a large cast, which he was resting on a stool.

Peter looked around him. Kate was queuing up with her friends to get a balloon animal, and Maggie was wiping ice cream off Eamon's chin.

He knew what he had to do.

'Be brave,' he whispered to himself.

Pulling on Blue's lead, he took a deep breath and made his way over to where Simon was seated. Along with boys from their class, there were others whom Peter didn't recognise – they must be Simon's friends from Dublin.

'Does it hurt?' Seamus Tallan asked, tapping the cast with a used candy floss stick.

'How much blood was there?' asked Trevor, Simon's best friend.

Simon was grinning, happy that all his friends were there. But his grin suddenly faded as he saw Peter and Blue approach. In fact, things went very quiet very quickly.

The rest of the boys looked at one another, not sure what to do or how to react.

'Who's that?' asked Trevor.

'That's Peter Farrelly,' answered Seamus.

'Eh, hello,' Peter said nervously.

'Hi,' said Simon, who also sounded a little bit nervous.

'How do you feel?' Peter tried again.

'Ok,' was the reply.

'This is a bit awkward,' Trevor whispered to Seamus, who nodded in agreement.

By now Blue had had enough. She had been sitting politely without getting even the smallest bit of attention. Her tail thumped the ground. She looked at Peter and then at Simon before finally tugging and pulling Peter in Simon's direction.

'No, Blue ...' Peter tried to hold her back, but it was no good. Blue had ideas of her own.

She jumped up onto Simon's lap, resting her two front paws on his good leg and sniffing the bandage on his head before giving him one of her infamous super wet, super sloppy licks.

The boys in the group stood back. There was no way Simon Sinclair was going to like this.

'Blue!' Peter said through gritted teeth. He was terrified she was going to hurt Simon, and then who knows what Simon would do to Peter.

But Simon's face broke into a huge grin and then the biggest fit of giggles ever. The sound of his giggles was all the encouragement Blue needed, and she licked and nudged Simon even more before finally stepping down, satisfied that she had loved this human sufficiently. She sat beside Peter, her long tongue hanging down and her tail moving from side to side. She was absolutely delighted with herself.

'I'm soaked,' laughed Simon. 'You are such a good dog. C'mere, Blue, c'mere.'

Blue couldn't believe her luck. This time, Peter didn't try to hold her back. Once again, she jumped up onto Simon's lap and nuzzled her head into his neck. Simon held her there for a short while, resting his own head on hers and putting his arms around her.

'You are the best dog,' he whispered again, looking into her eyes. 'Thank you, Blue, thank you for coming back to get me.'

'I don't know why you would want to get away from this place,' said Jake, another of Simon's Dublin friends. 'This place is brilliant.'

'Yeah, there's so much space, and did you see the cows and sheep in the field?' exclaimed Trevor.

'Oh, that will be Hazel Tree Farm,' explained Simon. 'That's where Peter and Blue live.'

'Wow!' came the collective gasp, followed by a chorus of 'Can we visit?' 'Can we pet a sheep?' 'Would a cow bite?'

Simon and Peter laughed at the questions.

Simon reached into his jacket pocket and took out a black marker. 'The doctor told me I could get my friends to sign my cast,' he said.

'I'll do it!' said Seamus Tallan.

'No, me first,' said Tommy, trying to push past him.

'No, it should be me, his best friend!' exclaimed Trevor.

'No,' said Simon. 'I would like Peter to be first. And Blue too, if you think she can.'

'Does that mean we're' – Peter was nearly afraid to say it – 'friends?'

'If that's ok with you,' answered Simon, a bit shyly. 'I understand if you don't want to be. I mean, after everything I did, how I was so …'

'Mean?' answered Seamus.

'A bully?' added Tommy.

'Yes,' said Simon. 'Both of those things.'

Thinking for a minute, Peter took the marker off Simon. He signed his name right on the front, where everyone could see. He then handed the marker to Blue, who took it in her mouth before moving her head and doing a small scribble of her own.

'She did it!' laughed Simon. 'She actually did it!'

The boys laughed and took turns to rub Blue before making way for the others to sign the cast.

'I'm back to school on Monday,' Simon told Peter. 'Mum says I might need a tutor to help me catch up.'

'I can come over after school and help if you like.' The words were out of Peter's mouth before he knew it.

What am I saying? Am I actually volunteering to hang out with Simon Sinclair, on purpose?

His tummy began fluttering again. What a stupid thing to say. It was positively the worst idea EVER!

'You would?' Simon sounded shocked. 'You would do that, for me?'

Peter nodded his head. 'Yeah, I guess so,' he replied. 'On one condition. As a friend, I get to play some of your video games. I assume you have *Motor Mash V* and *Splatoon*?'

'Deal.' Simon smiled.

The smell of the popcorn was making Peter's mouth water. Tugging at Blue's lead, he made his way over to get some.

'Hey, Peter,' Simon called after him.

Peter stopped and turned around.

'I'm sorry for taking the ball,' Simon said.

'I'm sorry for hitting you,' said Peter.

'Friends?' asked Simon.

'Friends,' answered Peter.

The flutters in Peter's tummy were gone. Maybe he and Simon could be friends. Maybe not best friends, but they could be friends, and that was a good place to start.

The party was a wonderful success. As guest of honour, Blue was presented with an enormous bone which she held proudly in her mouth for all to see. The Sinclairs had organised a photographer to come and take a picture of 'Blue the Hero'. Simon beckoned to Kate and Peter to get in the picture too.

'Blue will be a total diva by the end of this,' laughed Mam.

All too soon, it was time to go. Gathering their coats and jackets, Eamon, Maggie and the Farrellys made their way to the entrance.

'Eamon Cooper,' cried Maggie, 'is that another ice-cream cone I see?'

'Maybe it is' – Eamon shrugged his shoulders – 'maybe it isn't.'

'I am never eating again ...' groaned Kate.

'David, Marian!' Derek Sinclair came running up to them.

'I'm glad I caught you. Could I have a word, please, in my office?'

Feeling a little unsettled, Mam and Dad joined Derek in his office. Maggie, Eamon, Peter and Kate listened at the door, which was left slightly ajar.

'That TV project in America has been a total bust,' said Derek sadly. 'However, I have the most wonderful idea for a new show, and I believe Hazel Tree would be the perfect location.'

Dad and Mam looked at each other, not sure what Derek was talking about.

He tried again. 'I was wondering if you would be interested in allowing Hazel Tree Farm to be the location for a new TV programme I am looking to produce?'

SQUEAK!

The door edged open a little more as four sets of ears (five including Blue's) tried to hear the answer.

'I'm not sure I understand,' Dad said.

'Yes, what do you mean exactly?' Mam asked.

'Well, we would be filming a few days a week for about five months,' answered Derek. 'We would make sure not to get in the way of your farm work, and I can promise you a generous fee for the use of your property.'

'How generous?' Dad whispered, leaning forward.

SQUEEEEEAAAAKKK!

The 'ears' moved in closer.

The children couldn't hear Derek's answer, but by the way Eamon spluttered his fourth ice cream, they guessed that he had heard it – and that it was very generous indeed.

Mam put her hand to her mouth, and Dad put his hand to his forehead.

'That sounds good to us, Derek,' Dad said with a huge smile. 'Very good indeed.'

Epilogue

'This is Kate Farrelly signing off for another edition of *Zoo Files*.'

Using her hairbrush as a microphone, Kate practised her 'TV voice'. 'Hey Peter!' she called to her brother. 'What's my best angle?'

'The back of your head,' came the reply from the corridor. Peter ran down the stairs, narrowly avoiding the hairbrush that was flying his way.

As the winter months rolled in, Hazel Tree was beginning an exciting new chapter. Producers and camerapeople had arrived to pick suitable locations for the new SoFun show *Magnus Dean: Farmer By Day, Superhero By Night*. Filming was due to start in the summer, which was perfect as lambing would be complete and the landscape would be at its most beautiful.

The fee offered to the Farrellys for the use of their farm would be more than enough to cover the losses from this year's sheep sales, and there was still enough left over to …

'… buy more cows?' asked Dad.

'No!' said Mam. 'We are saving it.'

The Sinclairs had arranged for Kate and her bee garden to be featured on *Zoo Files*. Its presenter, Blake Wells, would be coming to film in the spring. Kate knew she was the one being interviewed, but she couldn't help but wonder what it would be like to be a TV presenter herself one day.

'Come on, Peter,' Mam called. 'Simon is here.'

Peter ran outside as Simon hopped out of his mother's car. The boys gave each other a fist pump before running behind the house to the paddock where 1360 and the (nearly grown) heifer calves were grazing.

'Homework first, you two,' laughed Diane. 'That's the rule.'

True to his word, Peter had helped Simon with his school-work, and in no time he had caught up with his class. Now Simon visited Hazel Tree any chance he got just to help out. He thought that maybe one day he could become a farmer like Eamon.

Maggie and Eamon had also presented Simon with something he never had but really needed.

Excitedly he ripped off the paper and opened the large white box to reveal a brand-new pair of wellington boots.

'No more of those fancy shoes when you visit Hazel Tree!' said Eamon. 'Now you can call yourself a real farmer.'

Calf 1360 mooed when she saw the boys approach with the meal bucket. Simon extended his hand to her and smiled as she nudged him and licked his jacket.

Dad and Eamon watched the boys at work. An earlier scan on the flock of sheep had shown the news they were hoping for: all the ewes were expecting little ones. It was going to be a busy lambing season.

'Who would have believed how our luck would change?' Dad said to Eamon, remembering the day when the calves arrived.

Eamon was about to answer when suddenly Dad's phone rang.

'Hello,' he answered. 'Eoin Bedford! Great to hear from you. How's farming college?'

Eamon turned back to keep an eye on the boys as Dad spoke to Eoin.

'Yes, absolutely.' Dad's voice sounded excited. 'That would be no problem at all. Tell them to call me.'

Dad hung up the phone, still staring at the screen. 'That was Eoin Bedford. He's away studying at the agricultural college.'

'What did he want?' Eamon asked.

Dad's face broke into a large smile. 'The college was hoping Hazel Tree might be able to offer some work experience to the students. They will pay us for our time, and we will have students working with us.'

Eamon grinned from ear to ear. Between TV shows, calves, lambs, and now teaching, the future was certainly looking bright.

'That was something my father always hoped to do,' Dad

said, his eyes shining. 'Find a way to spread the good farming practices of Hazel Tree.'

As Dad rang Mam to deliver the good news, Eamon could hear shrieks of joy on the other end.

He looked over at Peter and Simon as they watched the heifers enjoy their evening meal, Blue sitting attentively beside them. Simon had really come into his own, and the joy on his face when he was around animals told Eamon that he might be a farmer in the making.

Eamon was proud to be a part of this wonderful moment. He looked around the yard and the paddocks. It was truly a magical place.

Feeling the winter chill whip around his ears and the back of his neck, Eamon lifted his collar and pulled his hat down over his ears. He knew this land would never let them down.

'As I've always said,' he whispered under his breath, 'Hazel Tree always provides.'

obrien.ie/hazel-tree-farm

Hazel Tree Farm
Blue the Brave

Peter is hard at work training sheepdog Blue for the trials at
the Ballynoe Fair, while Kate – who wants to be a vet like
her mam – is busy with her cheeky pet hen, Hettie.
The first book in the Hazel Tree Farm series, following the
adventures of the Farrelly family, their neighbours, and a host
of furry, woolly and feathery friends!

Growing up with

tots to teens and in between

Why CHILDREN love O'Brien:

Over 350 books for all ages, including
picture books, humour, fiction, true stories,
nature and more

Why TEACHERS love O'Brien:

Hundreds of activities and teaching guides,
created by teachers for teachers,
all FREE to download from obrien.ie

Visit, explore, buy
obrien.ie